Whimsy

A Literary Doom & Gloom Antidote

Christine Boyer

Andrea Chesman

Anthony C. Ermi

Augusto Luiz Facchini

Michael Heyman

Jenn Hopkins

David Kirk

Xinyuan Shi

Leora Spitzer

J.J. Stewart

Sandra Unerman

T.J. Young

INK ALCHEMY
BOOKS

AN INK ALCHEMY BOOKS ORIGINAL

Compilation copyright © 2025 by Ink Alchemy Books

Trade Paperback ISBN: 979-8-9906798-3-2
eBook ISBN: 979-8-9906798-4-9

Library of Congress Control Number: 2025900314

Cover Art by Tanya Nicolaeva
Illustrations by David Kirk

inkalchemybooks.com

For my writing group gals:
bright spots in dark times.
—CHRISTINE BOYER

For Richard Ruane, whose song,
"I Know Stories," inspired my story.
—ANDREA CHESMAN

For the sake of optimism.
—ANTHONY C. ERMI

To my father, whose dedication to his family
made it possible for me to pursue writing.
—AUGUSTO LUIZ FACCHINI

For Sayoni, who brought me to Chail
and taught me Wrong Cricket.
—MICHAEL HEYMAN

To my kind-hearted fairies,
Violet, Primrose, and Wisteria.
—DAVID KIRK

To my family: thank you
for entertaining some crazy ideas.
—XINYUAN SHI

To my partner who is endlessly curious
about the universe around her.
—J.J. STEWART

For my family and
the Middleoak writing group.
—SANDRA UNERMAN

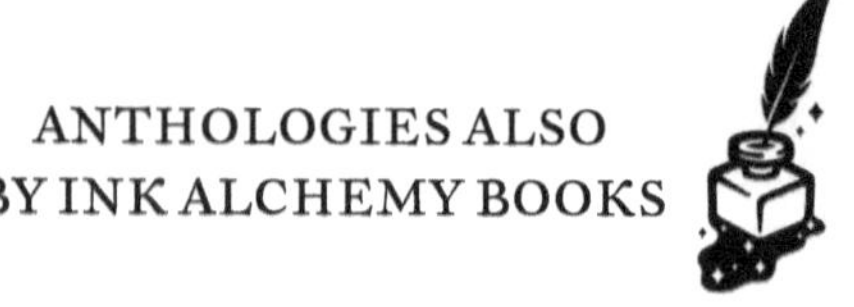

ANTHOLOGIES ALSO BY INK ALCHEMY BOOKS

Shift, 2024

Beware the Light: An Anthology of Dark Fiction, 2024

Contents

EDITOR'S FOREWORD

Naomi Artemi

Everybody looks at the family members of the departed at a funeral. They look and think, *How tragic for them.* They look and think, *Thank goodness that's not me.* At the funeral of my grandmother's best friend, I thought, *What a pretty bow.* It was a periwinkle velvet and was tying up the high ponytail of said departed's daughter. The ribbon was left long so that its ends brushed the shoulders of her tasteful black dress; too tasteful to belong to a twenty-something. It must have been her mother's. I remember little of the funeral other than that bow. It was a real, "Girls in white dresses with blue satin sashes," burst of cheerfulness at an otherwise grim occasion.

I overheard the daughter explain that it was how her mother used to style her hair as a girl. Because a bow at a funeral, apparently, needs justification. No one could say outright that it was inappropriate, as she was the grieving daughter. But had I worn the bow? Did whimsy have a place at such a somber affair?

I thought about that bow for a long time afterwards. Years. Then, as with all details from the past, eventually the image got misplaced somewhere in the muddle of memory, shoved into the junk drawer of my mind along with my fourth-grade teacher's name and how to play The Brandenburg Concerto No. 3 on second violin. And so, I had not given that bow a thought for almost as long as I had, probably not since my grandmother's passing (I can't say "since my grandmother's funeral," because she opted to have a garden cocktail party with live jazz and open bar in lieu of open casket and mourners. She said she wanted us to throw a party that she would have liked to be at. A wildly generous last wish.) Then, first week of January 2024, the image of that periwinkle bow popped right back into my head and tied itself around my thoughts, double-knotted.

My yoga teacher had come to class with a bright red ribbon in her hair. A down for a hike in any weather kind of woman, I was compelled to ask her about the out-of-character accessory.

"Oh!" she enthused, "I picked a word for the new year. Something I'm trying to invite more of into my life."

(A writer always has to ask.) "What word?"

"Whimsy."

The word itself likely originated as, "whim-wham," an early 17th century term for a trinket. It has evolved to include more than quaint and decorative objects, but quaint and decorative ideas, as well. Descriptors from a variety of definition sources: fanciful, playful, imaginative, magical, delightful, dreamlike, fairylike, enchanting, charming, quaint, quirky, unusual, surreal, wondrous, frivolous . . . However you choose to define it, "whimsy" has an ephemeral quality. It only exists in contrast to the mundane—the tedious to-do lists, the routines of repetition, scheduling time for taxes. If mundane were an ice cream flavor, it would be: Humdrum Vanilla (with stale oatmeal cookie chunks!). Whimsy, therefore, is to the daily grind as a bouquet of fresh flowers is to a meadow in winter. And much like the fleeting beauty of flowers, whimsy is such a rare day-to-day occurrence, that it has taken on an almost fabled status akin to Sasquatch sightings. How often do we encounter whimsy in the wild? But, in popular culture, it can become a phenomenon! *Alice in Wonderland, Mary Poppins, The Princess Bride, Howl's Moving Castle, Edward Scissorhands, James and the Giant Peach,* are some examples, to name but a few. The song, "What Does the Fox Say?" is an example of collective cultural whimsy that demonstrates demand. But someone has to start the whimsical snowball rolling . . .

The writers in this book, are those someones!

Of theses stories, some, such as *Mr. Spittleberg Serves the Two Sisters Tea* and *Felicia and the Baron,* are silly and light. Others—*She Who Destroys, Voyage Story*—touch on somewhat bleaker themes. But the ribbon that ties them all together is the feeling you get when you've finished reading one: warm and optimistic. Every single story in this collection concludes with a hopeful or uplifting ending.

But that's not real life! you protest.

But could it be? I counter.

Can whimsy be aspirational?

One might argue that current affairs demand that we not pull the wool (cap with pom-pom) over our eyes, that now is not the time to be frivolous with our attention. In defense of nonsense, there is a difference between seeking the positive and ignoring the negative. In support of whim and celebration of wham, this book is not a rejection of the undesirable and uncomfortable, it's a way to find the hope in the face of those things. Toxic positivity is being willfully ignorant. Pragmatic positivity is when we know the odds are against us, but we still *choose* hope. We know the flowers will wilt but we still go through the trouble of arranging them in a vase on the table. Why bother, when we know the display will be fleeting? Many a philosopher has expounded upon this question, most landing on some deep insight into the purpose of life. But maybe it's as simple as: pretty flowers make things not feel so bad.

When the dog bites, when the bee stings
When I'm feeling sad
I simply remember my favorite things
And then I don't feel so bad

Sometimes when life turns on us and bites, when living in the world stings like hell, and we are grieving our loss of innocence, we need to invite in those things that make us not feel so bad. Inviting the whimsical into your life is self-care. A bubble-bath for your brain! So, put googly eyes on your Roomba. Sleep in the canopy bed of your childhood dreams. Sing along with Julie Andrews in "The Sound of Music!"

Raindrops on roses and whiskers on kittens
Bright copper kettles and warm woolen mittens
Brown paper packages tied up with strings
These are a few of my favorite things

Wear the bow.

In a world of deadlines and adulting, fanciful is a stand against dull. Silly is an act of rebellion. Frivolity is a way to invite more joy into this world that is so often filled with the opposite. Imagination is a profound decision not to give up play as a "grownup." Whimsy is a flashlight in the dark, a beacon of optimism in soul-desiccating circumstances.

"Everything can be taken from a man but one thing: the last of the human freedoms—to choose one's attitude in any given set of circumstances, to choose one's own way. When we are no longer able to change a situation, we are challenged to change ourselves." The man who said that was Viktor Frankl. He was passionate about teaching his fellow humans that, even in the most dire of situations, one can always choose a positive attitude and find the silver lining in suffering. He was also a concentration camp survivor.

The 14th Dalai Lama who was exiled from his homeland of Tibet, has said as much: "Optimism doesn't mean that you are blind to the reality of the situation. It means that you remain motivated to seek a solution to whatever problems arise." Or my favorite: "Choose to be optimistic, it feels better."

There is a Vajrayana Buddhist teaching that positive thoughts and emotions can be antidotes to negative ones. If one thought can be an antidote to another, can the imagination be an antidote for despair? Can whimsy be the antidote for doom and gloom? When the woman wearing a bow at a funeral said that her mother always did her hair like that when she was a little girl, was that memory of a joyful moment medicine for her grief?

"Darkness cannot drive out darkness, only light can do that. Hate cannot drive out hate; only love can do that." MLK, Jr.

In other words, poison cannot cure poison. Only an antidote can. Like the one in your hands.

There is an argument for the power of whimsy as a political act: "yarn bombing" ugly urban settings, organizing social change through craftivism, videos of crocheted frogs baking in aprons to counteract internet toxicity, calendars of squirrels wearing hats as a stand against the stress of modern-day schedules, public sidewalk chalk art to bring a smile to people stuck on the work/errand treadmill. Spreading whimsy spreads hope. And we need hope that things can change, otherwise we will give up. And if we give up, the whimsy nay-sayers win!

My hope for you, dear reader who lives in this wonky, overwhelming, and often dreadful world, is that each of these dozen stories can invite in a little delight and a touch of light into these dark times. The real world is rough right now; we need escapism! Use this anthology as a literary doom and gloom antidote on those days that you need a glimmer. May that glimmer shine hope on others quailing in the dark. May this book inspire you to commit your own random act of whimsy. A bow in your hair, perhaps? Or for the daring; a bow tie!

And be careful with the news, will you?

SOSI'S WINGS

David Kirk

Fairies are heavy sleepers, so it wasn't until her nightdress was soaked through that Sosi sat up with a shiver. Icy water dripped steadily through a crack in the ceiling, splashing at the foot of her thistledown bed. "That patch was supposed to last the winter," she grumbled, peering at the garden through a hole in her flowerpot home. The mist rising from the last heaps of snow couldn't hide the mud and dead leaves of March. A single crocus bowed wearily under the weight of the raindrops. Sosi sighed, "And so it must be spring."

She settled on a nutshell to dry her feet with a blade of grass. There was nothing in the world Sosi hated so much as wet toes, but lately, it seemed they were wet all the time. Life hadn't always been like this. Not so long ago, she would winter with friends in a warm, southern meadow. There, the sun shone happily on fields ripe with flowers and sweet berries. Sosi had often grown so plump that it was difficult to fly north again! But now, the other fairies went without her. Since her accident, Sosi's old friends ignored her even when they were here.

"What do we have in common now?" they'd laugh.

It was mean. They were the ones who'd told her she could out-fly that wicked cat! Sosi reached beneath her sodden nightdress, scratching the nubs on her shoulders where wings had once been. She used to wish with all her heart that they would grow back. But since a fairy's magic resides in her wings, her wishing went for nothing. Now she wondered if it would have been better had the cat just finished her.

March passed. As the weather improved, so did Sosi's spirits. She hired the moles to repair her roof, and with her tiny pocket knife, she made pretty boots to keep her feet dry. One morning after a spring shower, she carefully laced her new boots and stepped out to admire the garden. Raindrops hung glistening from the leaves, and the rain-washed air seemed charged with the promise of good things to come. She lay down in a ray of sunshine atop a fragrant petal. A group of green caterpillars nibbled nearby. How she envied them. It wouldn't be long before they had wings of their own. Her eyelids grew heavy as the lullaby of their steady munching lulled her to sleep. She had a lovely dream. She sailed through the clouds on delicate butterfly wings—wings even more beautiful than those she had lost. How the other fairies admired her. How they envied her magnificent wings!

Sosi woke to familiar voices. "What kind of creature is that?" someone squawked.

"It's something like a fairy," barked another, but so bony and pale and with those awful green boots!" Sosi opened her eyes to see Teasel and Prig, two old fairy friends. Fresh back from the southern meadow, they were nicely plump, their skins golden from sunshine. They recognized her at last.

"Oh Sosi!" squealed Teasel, "We didn't know it was you! You're so thin. Have you been ill?"

"You should have come south with us!" scolded Prig.

Teasel laughed, "How could she, you silly bug? She hasn't any wings!" And with that, they flitted gaily into the garden.

Sosi fought back tears. She simply couldn't live another winter in that dreary flowerpot. She must have wings! If only she still had her magic. In desperation, she silently formed the secret words she'd learned as a child, "Kalaata . . . Mela . . . Zephyra . . . Zoot." She squeezed her eyes shut and imagined beautiful wings extending from her shoulders. Yes! They were growing. She could feel it. She could feel it! Her fingers reached eagerly to her shoulder blades. Nothing . . . But how could she concentrate with those awful caterpillars and their hideous munching!

Now, there was another noise. Sploop, sploop, sploop . . . Splut! A drop of water exploded against her petal. It nearly splashed her new boots! She looked up. Water trickled over the side of a cupped leaf. As she edged away, higher branches came into view. At the very top of the plant, a caterpillar poised on a twig as if about to jump from a high dive. "NOOOO!" Sosi shouted, but too late. The fat caterpillar dropped down, down, down, flopping belly first into the rain-filled leaf. For a terrible moment, the leaf sagged dangerously. Then it tipped, and a great gush of water slapped Sosi from her perch and into the wet grass below.

Dragging herself onto her elbows, Sosi found the caterpillar twisted across her knees. It choked up water, sputtering excitedly,

"I think I flew that time. You saw me, didn't you?" Cold water dribbled down Sosi's legs and into her new boots. With a bitter sob, she tumbled the caterpillar onto the grass, untied a wet boot, and cast it gloomily into a puddle. "What lovely boots," coughed the caterpillar. Sosi stopped crying and gazed doubtfully at her remaining boot.

"Really?" she sniffed. "You don't think they're awful?"

"Oh no, indeed," said the caterpillar. "They're only the prettiest boots I've ever seen." He ducked into the puddle, spreading ripples as he made his way across. A moment later he returned with the discarded boot, offering it up with such ceremony that it made Sosi smile just a little. She extended her hand and gently shook one of his foremost legs.

"I'm called Sosi," she said. "And what is your name?"

"Me?" he sighed, "I haven't got a name." Sosi peered at him through narrowed eyes, considering as she shook out her soggy boot.

"I'll call you Gabriel," she pronounced. The caterpillar looked pleased.

"You don't think it's too grand for me?" he asked.

"Much too grand," laughed Sosi, "So you'll just have to grow into it, won't you?" Sosi got to her feet. "It was very nice to meet you, Gabriel," she said. Gabriel looked at her with great concern.

"I'm sorry to have made you wet," he said. "Will you be alright?"

"Oh, I'm better now," said Sosi. "I wasn't crying because I was wet. I just miss flying with the other fairies sometimes." She gestured to her back. "I've lost my wings, you see."

Gabriel was stricken.

"You had wings and then had them taken away?" he gasped, "How can you bear it?"

"I can't," said Sosi.

"I'm so sorry," Gabriel said. "I can imagine how beautiful it must be to soar across the meadows, to glide among the treetops, to sail the clouds, but of course, imagine is all I *can* do. I'm starting to realize—caterpillars were simply never meant to fly. It's funny, because I was just wishing that someone would come along who'd understand about flying, and now here you are."

Sosi stared at him, dumbfounded. Didn't he know that he'd soon be a butterfly with wings of his own? Could he be so silly?

"But you . . ." An idea formed in Sosi's head even as she spoke. "But you . . . you'll . . ." It would be a mean trick, she knew. Still, she needed wings so very badly, and it almost seemed that this caterpillar was sent as the answer to her wish. Perhaps he only appeared here to deliver her wings! "But you'll need fairy magic if you want to fly!" she cried. "I can see that you are in need, so I'm going to grant you one wish! Remember, it's just one, so be sure to wish for the thing you want most in the world." Sosi knew very well what he'd say. He wanted wings. And why shouldn't she take advantage of that? After all, he didn't really even know what he was missing. Gabriel didn't disappoint her.

"Wings!" he cried, "I wish for wings!"

"Your wish shall be granted," said Sosi, bowing in a grand gesture. "By the way, you *do* know that you'll have to give something to earn your wish, don't you? Wishes don't come free."

Gabriel blinked. "But I have nothing."

"You will though," Sosi explained. "This is how it will work: I'll give you wings, you'll get to fly just as you've dreamed, then, at the end of summer, you'll give them back to me in payment for your wish. Is it a bargain?"

"I see," said Gabriel, looking so intensely into Sosi's eyes that she felt as though he might see right through her. "You must want wings very, very badly." Sosi looked away.

"Is it a deal then?" she asked.

"Yes," said Gabriel quietly, "I want you to have my wings." With her hands, Sosi traced circles in the air above Gabriel's head, reciting the magic words,

"Kalaata . . . Mela . . . Zephyra . . . Zoot." She finished with a flourish, falling to her knees as if exhausted. Gabriel looked over his shoulder for his new wings. Sosi laughed. "You didn't think you'd get them just like that did you? Proper magic takes time!" Gabriel said it was an honor to help Sosi fly again, and for him, to have wings for even a day would be better than never to fly at all. Sosi felt a little guilty about tricking Gabriel out of the wings that were his birthright, but she put that out of her mind. There was work to do. If she was going to take his wings, they might as well be strong healthy ones. She meant to see that he got his vitamins.

She needn't have worried. Gabriel thrived in her company. As summer blossomed, he and his appetite grew. He could not stop talking about flying. "How high do you shupposhe I'll go?" he sputtered through a mouthful of milkweed, "opher sha clouds, you shink?" He swallowed and pointed upward with a stubby hand. "What's up there? Are there cloud meadows? What sorts of caterpillars live there and what do they eat? Does the milkweed float free, or is it rooted in the clouds?"

"Nobody lives up there," Sosi sighed, "And when you get your wings you'll be a good flyer but you cannot reach the clouds, so do not try! They are too far away." With a kick, she snapped a small pod from its stem and watched it bounce down the leaves to smack on the rocks below. "It isn't safe, and you're wearing me out just thinking of it." Gabriel raised an eyebrow, took another mouthful and chewed thoughtfully before bringing the subject down to earth.

"Have you noticed that the milkweed on this patch is sweeter than the milkweed near the oaks? I think it's the morning sun that bathes them here. It makes them . . . more cheerful." Sosi looked across the shining meadow to the shaded oaks. Her shoulders relaxed as she nibbled the tender end of a pod. It was sweeter. She was ever amazed at the variety and richness of Gabriel's knowledge. He saw so many things that she'd never noticed. He could tell you the name of any tree from the shape or taste of its leaves—knew each flower by its smell and color. He remembered the names of every insect he met and would greet them, always with a kind word. Though Sosi had begun trying to fatten Gabriel just to ensure he'd grow strong wings, it wasn't long before she was thinking only of pleasing him.

As she searched the garden, gathering the tenderest leaves for his meals, Gabriel watched Sosi too. How unlike other fairies she was. Never arrogant or vain, she seemed to consider him more than herself. She appreciated all the things that he pointed out to her—loved all that he loved. He knew well enough that she had stayed with him at first merely to protect her investment in his wings, but he believed that had now passed. She was his best friend and he was hers, though she might not yet know it.

It was nearly September, and Gabriel had become so plump that he tired even of eating. Hanging upside down over the edge of a leaf, he stared wearily at the horizon. "Time to sleep," he murmured. Sosi knew that his change was beginning.

"And when you wake," she whispered, "you'll fly at last." But Gabriel didn't hear her. He was already dreaming.

Sosi arranged her bed next to Gabriel's cocoon that night, but she could hardly sleep thinking of the wings that would soon be hers. With her lovely new wings she would fly with the fairies once more. That was why she found it perplexing when she realized it was no longer the fairies that she missed. It was Gabriel, three inches away, asleep in his cocoon. Gabriel seemed to understand her every thought, every feeling. And there was nothing he didn't know! Each day Sosi thought of a dozen important questions she wanted to ask him. *How does the rain find its way to the clouds? Where do the stars go during the day? How does a whole flower fit into a tiny seed?* She even surprised herself by discovering new wonders on her own; then she would ask herself, *What would Gabriel think?* It was then that her plan for Gabriel struck her as very wrong. It might be different if she actually had the magic to get him his wings, but since he was getting them anyway . . . and besides, he was the best friend she'd ever had, always kind, always thoughtful. Perhaps she didn't need those wings so badly after all. Maybe she would tell Gabriel to keep his wings.

Lonely weeks passed as Sosi continued her vigil by Gabriel's ripening cocoon. Its thinning membrane glistened in the starlight, revealing patterns in the delicate wings folded beneath. A chill in the night air heralded autumn's return. Sosi covered Gabriel with a leaf, snuggling against him to share her warmth.

Infused with a glow of security, Sosi knew that something wonderful had happened even before she opened her eyes. The leaf that had sheltered her was gone. In its place, a magnificent butterfly wing blanketed her. "Good morning," said Gabriel. Sosi sat up with a start.

"Gabriel?" she gasped. "Is it really you?" Gabriel fanned his wings.

"Your magic worked," he smiled. Sosi scooted back to admire his new form.

"They're the most beautiful wings I've ever seen," she sighed. "Have you tried them yet?"

Gabriel looked beyond Sosi to the open sky.

"I haven't dared," he stammered.

"But it's what you've been waiting for!"

"Yes, but what if I can't?" said Gabriel. "What if I don't know how?"

"You won't need to," laughed Sosi, "Your wings know the way." She led him to the edge of the leaf. Without another word he was in the air—soaring and swooping as if he'd flown all his life. Sosi watched proudly. Surely, no one had ever flown more gracefully. He sailed back and fluttered before her.

"It's better than I ever imagined!" he laughed. "I'm going to try a longer run. Wait for me!"

Sosi waited. She waited through the morning, and then through the afternoon. Once, she thought she saw Gabriel flitting across an open patch of sky, but she couldn't be sure. So many butterflies had emerged in the past few days, and from a distance, they all looked alike. Alone on her leaf again, Sosi had time to think. She wouldn't have believed it possible to feel so happy for someone else, yet so sorry for herself. Gabriel was her only friend. What if she never saw him again? And if she did, how could she explain about the other butterflies? Surely some of them were caterpillars he'd known. He would talk to them, and he would find out that they had all gotten their wings. He'd know she'd lied to him. Why would he ever come back then? And how could she blame him?

Gabriel did return, though the sun had nearly set when he lighted before her, flushed from the thrill of his first day of flight. "The world is a beautiful place," he whispered, then, folding his wings over Sosi, they both closed their eyes.

And so it went for the last weeks of summer. Gabriel departed every morning to explore the woods and meadows, coming back at sunset to tell Sosi of his adventures. Curled beneath the protection of his wings, she lived through Gabriel's stories, and in return told tales of the southern meadow that she'd loved for so many winters past.

One morning, Sosi woke alone. No strong wing sheltered her, in its stead, a dry leaf. No friend said a warm good morning. The silence was broken only by falling leaves. She sat up, looking amongst the nearly bare trees for a sign of her friend, when from the branches above there came a faint whispering. Gabriel was talking to another butterfly. She lay back down and pretended to sleep. She couldn't hear all that they said, but Gabriel's friend wasn't so quiet. She heard enough, ". . . shouldn't be listening to a lying fairy, especially a wingless . . . doesn't matter what you promised . . . you should be coming with us."

Soon the talking stopped. Sosi was alone. The day passed. She knew that winter was coming and she should prepare her flowerpot, but she couldn't face that—not just yet. The sun set. Gabriel did not return. She climbed to the branch where he had hung as a chrysalis just a few weeks before. She had thought she was lonely then, but she hadn't known what loneliness was. Gabriel's empty chrysalis still hung beneath its leaf, the last leaf on the tree. Sosi climbed into it and quickly fell asleep.

She had a terrible dream. Her flowerpot lay half buried beneath a bank of snow. Wind shrieked through open cracks. The door shuddered, then ripped from its hinges. Sosi lay frozen in her bed, unable to move. She had never felt so cold, and the wind kept shrieking, shrieking, shrieking.

Angry buzzing roused Sosi from her nightmare. Teasel and Prig hovered overhead. They scowled down at her, faces sour as crab apples. "You may not have wings," sneered Teasel, "but that's no reason you shouldn't behave like a fairy. You've spent so much time skulking around with that . . . that bug, that you've become one!"

"You don't deserve to fly south!" snorted Prig in disgust. "You're not one of us anymore. It's a wonder you ever had wings!" The cruel pair disappeared into the southern sky, leaving Sosi shivering in despair.

But there was no time for feeling sorry for herself. Winter was coming, and Sosi knew that if she was going to survive, she would need to hurry. She climbed down from the tree and made for her abandoned flowerpot. It was worse than she'd expected. The cracks in the roof were huge, the floor, mud soup, the walls thick with mold. Breathing the dank air, Sosi's head swam. Outside, she found a rain-filled leaf and splashed her face to clear her head. It made her think of how she first met Gabriel. Where was he now when she needed him most? She gazed at her reflection in the water and tried to imagine that she wore wings once more. With eyes closed, and little hope, she wished as she'd never wished before, reciting the magic words, "Kalaata...Mela...Zephyra ...*Zoot!*" Then, gazing into the pool, she was astonished to see beautiful wings rising behind her.

"I'm back," said Gabriel.

"Oh," said Sosi sadly. "It's you. Of course, it's you. I thought...just for a second that the wings were mine. I should've known better. It's never so easy working magic on yourself."

So this, thought Sosi, was how her magic was meant to work after all. She'd wished for wings and Gabriel had appeared once more.

"I didn't want to take your wings," she said, "not anymore. But it's the only way I can live. Everybody deserves to live." She opened her pocket knife. "You can stay here for the winter. It just needs to be aired a bit. Are you ready then?" Wiping tears from her eyes, Sosi cut through the delicate structure at the base of Gabriel's wings. With great care, Gabriel sewed his severed wings to Sosi's shoulders.

"They look beautiful on you," he said, but Sosi was already gone.

She flew as if she could escape her guilty conscience, blinded by tears as she raced to find her fairy friends. Angry chatter rippled the air as she neared the southbound fairies. Teasel, Prig, and a plump fairy named Xyla were arguing bitterly over which of them had the prettiest wings. As Sosi fluttered into view, the contest became pointless. Their faces fell.

"She stole that butterfly's wings!" scowled Prig. "Not fair! Now I won't be the prettiest."

"You weren't the prettiest anyhow!" scolded Xyla, giving Prig a shove. "It's me who isn't the prettiest anymore!"

Teasel laughed, "And all summer we thought you spent your time with that worm because you liked him. We never guessed you were just after his wings! I didn't think you had it in you. How did you manage it?"

Sosi explained their bargain.

"You paid him by letting him use his own wings for a little while?" squealed Prig. "And I said you weren't anything like a fairy! You're brilliant! Where is he now?"

"Well, he can't fly south," stammered Sosi guiltily. "So I gave him my flowerpot to live in."

"You are SO fairy," grinned Teasel, "because when we come back in the spring, it'll be *your* flowerpot again. Butterflies can't stand the cold. He'll never survive the first snow!"

Sosi's face turned white. What had she done? She'd betrayed her only friend and these fairies were congratulating her. With three beats of her wings, she had turned and was racing north. The other fairies forgot about her instantly. Their voices tinkled against the cold air like broken glass as each insisted that she was the prettiest once more.

Gabriel was staring out of the broken window of his dreary new home when Sosi fluttered into the doorway. "I lied to you," she whispered, shrinking back as Gabriel turned. "Please don't look at me," she stammered. "I couldn't stand it if you looked at me." Gabriel turned back to the window and Sosi continued, "I'm not a magic fairy. A fairy's magic is in her wings, so when mine were ripped off . . . I tried to convince myself that my magic was back and that you only existed because I wished for wings, but that was just to make myself feel better about tricking you. I knew it was wrong. I knew all along."

"No," said Gabriel, shaking his head.

"It's true," said Sosi. "You were getting those wings anyway. All caterpillars get them. I cheated you out of your wings."

"I know that," sighed Gabriel. "I just meant the wishing part was wrong. It wasn't your wish that brought us together." He turned now to look at Sosi. "It was mine."

"But caterpillars don't have magic," protested Sosi. "Do they?"

Gabriel smiled sadly, "How did you suppose we caterpillars get our wings?" Sosi stared at the floor as Gabriel went on. "I wished for someone who'd understand me—somebody who knew what it was to fly. Then, when you told me your story, I felt so sorry. I wanted you to fly again. To lose one's wings is—it's just too sad."

"But you gave up yours," Sosi whispered. Gabriel was silent. Sosi took the knife from her pocket. She cut the threads binding the stolen wings to her shoulders, and with trembling hands, sewed them to Gabriel's back. With the last stitch in place, the seam disappeared before her eyes. Brittle leaves rustled through the open door on a chill breeze.

"It's going to be winter again soon, Sosi coughed. You need to fly south now, and I need my house back." Gabriel stood to face her.

"You'll be alright?" he asked.

"I'll be fine," said Sosi without confidence. "The last two winters were so cold, this one is sure to be milder."

From the doorway, Gabriel looked back for the last time into Sosi's dreary flowerpot. "Before I go," he said, "I can see that you're in need, so I'm going to grant you one wish. Remember, it's only one, so be sure to wish for the thing you want most in the world."

Sosi smiled, recognizing her own words. She thought for a moment, studying the play of sunlight shimmering across Gabriel's wings.

"I wish that you would forgive me," she said. "I wish that you would still be my friend."

"You don't wish for wings?" asked Gabriel. Sosi shook her head.

"Flying isn't as important as I thought."

"Your wish shall be granted," said Gabriel. But you know, wishes don't come free. You'll have to give something to earn your wish."

Sosi looked around the damp, crumbling walls of her neglected flowerpot. "I have nothing," she said sadly.

Gabriel knelt beside her and took her shivering fingers in his.

"Far to the south," he said, "there's a beautiful meadow I've heard of. The sun shines every day over fields of flowers and ripe berries. Climb on my back my friend. As payment for your wish, I'll need you to show me the way."

Many summers have passed since Sosi discovered that the wings she loved best came with a friend she loved even more. The next time you see a butterfly flitting gaily among the flowers or along a wooded lane, look carefully. It may be Gabriel and Sosi, together still, sailing happily wherever warm breezes blow.

THE ADVENTURES OF WAYFARER DOCK AND IN-BETWEEN

Xinyuan Shi

A lot of strange people lived in Wayfarer Dock, but the strangest by far was Mr. Baz. He lived in a little beachfront house that smelled of seagull droppings and dried seaweed. It was painted white with no shutters and tinted windows, much to the dismay of his curious neighbors.

Mr. Baz didn't often leave his house, but when he did, it was always precisely at 12:00 pm on a Sunday afternoon, and he would go to the only department store in town. There, he would buy ruby red paint (the kind that doesn't leave a glossy surface), three paint rollers, five candelabra candlesticks (the unscented kind), and a bag of cat food (chicken flavored, not beef). Mr. Baz didn't possess a car, so he would carry his newly bought items on his shoulders or in three paper bags (he was an environmentalist—at least when it came to plastic waste—global warming just made the world more comfortable as far as he was concerned), and would arrive back at home before the town clock tower could ring twice.

Sometimes, his neighbors would pass him on the street and say a pleasant greeting to which Mr. Baz would nod in acknowledgement of but never return. That was fine by his neighbors. They had long since decided that Mr. Baz was a taciturn man, and thus left him alone. After all, each of them had their own secrets and knew the value of a nose that wasn't nosy. That did not mean that they weren't curious. Speculations abounded about Mr. Baz's past, the reason behind his peculiar Sunday routine, and, above all, what he did in that house of his.

The first thing that he did was quite ordinary by the standards of his neighbors. Mr. Baz ate. For three meals a day, he ripped open the cat food bag, took out a handful of dried pellets and stuffed them down his unhinged jaw. There was never a crumb left, he ate so well.

The second thing that Mr. Baz did was, admittedly, less ordinary. He painted. No landscapes or portraits, abstracts or anything of the sort that resembles human art. Instead, Mr. Baz's art came in the form of a pentagon, stark red against the layers of faded pentagons on his living room floor. He was a perfectionist, so each side of the pentagon was exactly two feet, and each angle was not a degree shy of seventy-two. Sometimes, if Mr. Baz felt like adding a flair to his art, he would set an odorless candelabra candlestick at each corner of the pentagon, and, snapping the fingers of his left hand—*snap, snap, snap, snap, snap*—would light each wick, one after the other. His tinted windows didn't let in much sunlight, so the flickering flames were the only things to see by, not that Mr. Baz needed them to see in the dark.

When his eating and his painting were finished, Mr. Baz did

his third and least ordinary thing. He spoke, but his speaking wasn't done in English, Spanish, French, Mandarin, Arabic, German, Afrikaans, or in any other conceivable human language. No, Mr. Baz was far more worldly than that, and so, he spoke in Tongues.

⠇ ⊿⊢z, ⠇ ⠶⊢z, ⠒ ⋯⊢Ŧ, •⊙ yo⟶ ∘◯∘⊶⊙∘ ℏ∘◯◯ ⊰ ℏ⊙⊙! Tℏ ⊱∘ ⊙◆' •∘◆• ∘ ℏ∘ℓ◯ ⊙ℓ⟩! The exact translation of Mr. Baz's words has been lost in the writing of this story, but the essence is something along the lines of: *Mr Raz, Mr. Maz, Ms. Lam, get your odoriferous hides up here! This fort isn't going to hold itself!* Of course, Mr. Baz said it in a much more delicate manner. He was an environmentalist *and* polite if nothing else.

And then, the strangest thing of all happened. The pentagon responded!

⠂∘□ ◆⊙⊙◯ ∘ ℏ∘□, Mr. Raz said in a voice that abraded the eardrums.

⊰⊙∘∘ℓ□ □ ∘ ◯∘◆□ ℏ⊢⊙ ∘ ℏ∘□, Mr. Maz said.

□⊙ ⇕⊢◆ ℏ⊙⊢ □∘∘ ⟩◆⊙□. Ms. Lam was the self-proclaimed mediator in the group and as such her voice was the loudest of all.

Mr Baz shook his head. "Really," he muttered under his breath. "Why must they take so long every single time?" Out loud, he said, ∘ℓ.

They exchanged a few more pleasantries, the majority of which was composed of news and the weather. ∩ ℏ⊢◯ ⇕⊙⊙◆ ⊢ ⊰⊢∘⇕ℓ⊢ℓy ⟩∘⊙y ⊙◯k. Tℏ⊙y ⇕∘ ⊙ ⊢ ⟩⊶y y⊙⊢ ⊙⇕∘⊙! When they had finished updating each other,

Mr. Baz snuffed out the candles with a sharp clap and scratched at the paint on the floor with a toenail until the pentagon had been broken. By that time, it was quite dark outside and, because even strange people like Mr. Baz needed sleep, he went to bed.

Angelique was an ill-fitting name for the eleven-year-old who lived four houses down from Mr. Baz. For one, Angelique was not angelic in the slightest and often got up to more trouble than Mr. Baz and his cohort combined. The slime decorating her bathroom toilet, the shredded egg cartons littering the neighborhood playground, and the half-cooked yolks splattered across the street all had Angelique's name proudly stamped on them. She wasn't a troublemaker though. Or rather, she didn't make trouble for trouble's sake. She did the things that she did because her nemesis was boredom and nothing vanquished boredom better than getting into trouble.

For another thing, Angelique didn't like her name. Angel or Angela or even Angelina would have been fine, but no, her parents just *had* to be creative and name her Angelique...So she told everyone to call her something else, and they decided on *Meep*.

Meep was rarely alone (getting into trouble was much more fun when your friends were involved as well) and she was often seen with Jordan (also known as Pez because of the candy he always carried in his pocket) and Laura (just Laura).

On that particular day, Meep's nemesis was rearing its ugly head again as they walked down their street, and Pez, having recognized the signs, was doing his best to brainstorm things to do. "Want to head to the beach? We can play some volleyball."

"We've already done that three times this week," Meep said around the apple she was currently devouring. It had been freshly picked from a neighbor's backyard and was green and sour, just the way Meep liked them.

"What about the playground?"

"We're banned, remember?" said Laura.

"No regrets." Meep threw her half-eaten apple to the ground and stomped on it, smearing juice and seeds onto the pavement.

"The mall?"

"Boring."

"We should stay inside," Laura said, shading her eyes with her hand. "It's too bright outside, and I'm burning."

"Meep," said Meep. She was prone to make that sound whenever she was surprised, disgusted, frustrated, depressed, happy, or really any emotion other than bored. "You need the sun. You're paler than chalk, no offense."

Laura, who wasn't offended in the slightest, shrugged.

"Then what do you want to do, Meep?" Pez threw up his hands in exasperation. He had known her for nearly his whole life and was well acquainted with her different moods, this one especially. He knew that the best way to handle them was to let Meep do what she wanted, as she inevitably did every time.

"Since you asked," she said, "There's this one thing I've been dying to do for awhile—"

"How can you do anything when you're dying?" Laura said.

"Not literally! I've wanted to look through Mr. Baz's house. He's always so secretive, who knows what he does in there? He could be a bounty hunter with a chest full of trophies or . . . a zoologist with a backyard unicorn!"

"Or," said Laura, "he could be a psychopath who kidnaps kids our age and keeps them locked up in his basement."

Pez blinked. "I think what Laura is trying to say is that it's not safe. People don't bother Mr. Baz for a reason, and it's probably a good one."

Meep had known Pez for just as long as he had known her and, just as he was well-acquainted with her different moods, she was well-acquainted with his. She knew that the best way to handle Pez when he was being disagreeable was to sidle up to his side, close like a starving caterpillar on a fat cabbage leaf, and look up (he was a lanky twelve-year-old boy) directly into his eyes. There was an expression that Meep used, forming her mouth and her cheeks just so and letting a glint enter her eyes that was half pleading and half sorrowful but wholly irresistible.

"Stop," Pez said, averting his eyes.

Meep cranked up the pleading and inserted a little into her voice. Pez was being especially difficult today. "*Please?* It'll be fun."

"I don't want to get into any more trouble."

"We won't. We can go when Mr. Baz is out. You know he leaves his house every Sunday around noon and isn't back until two. He'll never know."

"*I'll* know!"

"Meep, just add it to the list." Then, turning to Laura, she said, "Don't you think it'll be fun?"

Laura shrugged.

"See? She's with me. Come on, Pez, this can't be worse than that time we stole eggs from Laura's nan's chicken coop." Laura's nan, known in the neighborhood as Mrs. Coldstrome, was not your quintessential grandmother. She did not love to bake, nor were her fingers well-adjusted to knitting. She had the habit of wearing a hideously distracting chartreuse wig and kept a clowder of five cats which were fed chicken-flavored (not beef) cat food, and four laying hens in an outdoor coop. She was the only one in the neighborhood to keep chickens and was, as Meep thought of her, an *egg-cellent* supplier.

"Mrs. Coldstrome is a harmless old lady! Mr. Baz is . . . Mr. Baz!"

"*Exactly*," Meep said as if Pez had explained everything. "Let's go before he gets back." Then, grabbing his reluctant hand, Meep pulled him up the street to where Mr. Baz's white house stood. Laura followed along behind them like she always did.

At the very moment that Meep, Pez, and Laura were preparing to dive headfirst into prodigious trouble, Ms. Lam, Mr. Raz, and Mr. Maz were up to their own schemes in the In-Between. Things could have been going better, and Ms. Lam was particularly upset.

↦⌒◯≻ℓ ⌒•↦↦⌒◯□□ ↦⌒◯≻ℓ ⌒↦⌒◯≻ □ she boomed. Her voice was usually loud, but she had unhinged her jaw to give it an extra *oomph*. There are some things in the In-Between that do not bear translation. Ms. Lam's words are a prime example of that little fact, and we will leave them in their original text.

≰◯↦ℓℓy, ⋮ ⋯↦Ŧ, ⌒ ⌒ ◆⌒ ⌒ℏ ◆ℏ⌒◆•⌒◆ y⌒◯ℓ≻ ≻⌒ ≰⌒Ŧ≺ℓy ⌒≺◯◆ ↦◆⌒ℏ◯ ⌒◯⌒◆ ↦◆◯ ⌒◯ ⇕↦◆ •◯ ⌒◆ ⌒ℏ ℏ⌒◆• Mr. Raz's sandpaper voice scrapped out. *Really, Ms. Lam, it is not worth unhinging yourself for. Simply open another vein and we can get on with things.* (For the sake of the reader's understanding, we will endeavor to translate some of the In-Betweeners' script. For true understanding, the reader should endeavor to learn to speak in Tongues).

The source of Ms. Lam's ire, Mr. Maz, peeked sheepishly over his ochre-tipped fingernails. ⊰∘⌣y. *Sorry.*

⌐↦∙∙ y∘⌐ ⌐∘⌣y, y∘⌐ ∓∘∙⌐⊙-ℓ↦⇕ ∘◆∙, ⌐⊰∘◆⊙ℓ⊙⌐ ℓ⌐z! ∩ ⌐⊰⊙◆∙∙ ∙ℏ⊙ ⊙◆∙∘⌐⊙ ⊙⌐⊙ ℓ↦⇕∘⌐∘◆∙ ∘⌐⊙⌐ ∙ℏ∘ ⊰∘⌣∙∙ ↦◆⊙ y∘⌐ ⇕∘ℓ⊙◆'∙∙ ⊙⌐⊙◆ ⌐↦∙∙⇕ℏ y∘⌐ ⇕ℓ⌐⇕⇕⊙⊙ ⊱⊙⊙∙∙! *Eat your sorry, you mogre-lacking, spineless klutz! I spent the entire eve laboring over this port and you couldn't even watch your clubbed feet!* A mogre is a barnacle-like organism that attaches itself to the hide of some In-Betweeners. Although slightly para-sitic, the In-Betweeners treat them like a delicacy, plucking them off of acquaintances and adversaries alike and popping them into their mouths like popcorn. It tastes like chicken, if you were won-dering.

∩∙∙ ⌐↦∙⌐ ↦◆ ↦⇕⇕∘⊙⊙⊙◆∙∙, said Mr. Maz.

∩◆ ∙ℏ⊙ ∘◆∙∙⊙⌐⊙⌐∙∙∙∙ ∘⊱ ⌐⊰↦⌐∘◆∙. Suffice to say, Ms. Lam was murderously angry.

Mr. Raz, who was quite fond of Mr. Maz and at this moment quite afraid for his life, stepped in. He pushed Ms. Lam down so that her rump was nestled comfortably in the black sand. He waved Mr. Maz to the other side of the port, far from Ms. Lam, and said, ∩'ℓℓ ⊱∘⌐ ∙ℏ⊙ ⊰∘⌣∙∙∙∙ ∩ ℏ↦⌐∘⊙ ⊰ℓ⊙◆∙∙y ∘◆ ∓y ⌐∘∘◆∙∙ ▱∘⌐ ⌐∘∙ ⇕↦⇕ ↦◆⊙ ⌐⊙ℓ↦⌐∙, ⋮⌐∙ ∙∙∙↦∓∙ ⋮∙∙ ⋮↦z, ⌣y ◆∘∙∙ ∙∙∘ ⇕⌐⊙↦⌐∙∙ℏ⊙. *I'll fix the port. I have plenty in my veins. You sit back and relax, Ms. Lam. Mr. Maz, try not to breathe.*

Mr. Maz held his breath and turned purple—no need to be alarmed, that was his second typical color. Ms. Lam turned her head away and crossed her arms. She had not forgiven Mr. Maz but had decided she was no longer going to eat him that day.

Satisfied that he could turn his back on the two, Mr. Raz kneeled to inspect the port. It was ruby red like the paint that formed Mr. Baz's pentagon, but it wasn't paint. Ms. Lam had drawn an intricate pattern of shapes and swirls within shapes and swirls that would have been dizzying to the human eye. The effect however was ruined by the large smudge in the topmost corner where an octagonal shape met a swirl that looked like the inside of a conch shell. Mr. Raz wiped away the smudged part, making sure not to disturb the rest of the port. Then, with his needle-like fingers, he punctured his wrist and watched as viscous liquid dripped down his arm to collect in the palm of his other hand. When he had enough, Mr. Raz licked his wrist and arm clean, dipped his finger in the liquid, and began to draw.

First, Mr. Raz fixed the conch shell swirl. The lines that had been drawn in the sand had been done by Ms. Lam's thick, stubby fingers. His fingers were thin, so he had to go over the lines a dozen times to achieve the desired thickness. The viscous liquid went on the sand a rusted red but dried a bright ruby that matched the rest of the port. When Mr. Raz finished the swirl, he moved on to the octagon.

It was painstaking work. Ports were notorious for being simple in concept but difficult in practice. There were no set rules, only vague guidelines or fundamental principles that could be followed if an In-Betweener were so principled. If they were not, that did not preclude them from travel or communication. After all, it wasn't so long ago, at the height of the Great Fear, that there had been several In-Betweeners renowned for their ability to design ports following nothing but their expansive guts.

Mr. Raz was a principled In-Betweener and he swore by the fundamentals. The first of which was: distance equated to complexity, or the further one wanted to travel or communicate, the more complicated the design had to be. For instance, if Mr. Raz, Mr. Maz, and Ms. Lam were trying to travel to the Tartarian Pits, then the port would have been a simple oval inside a diamond inside another oval with a rectangular spiral just for flair (Ms. Lam was fond of her spirals). But the three were not trying to travel to the Tartarian Pits, and the destination they had in mind required a more intricate design. The second principle was simple: an unmatched port had a mind of its own. Creating a single port in isolation with itself was an exercise in randomness. If you had a strict destination, it was best for the port to be linked to another in the location you wanted to travel.

Mr. Raz finished fixing the octagon, added a few flairs of his own (he was a rhombus fan, himself), and then stepped back to admire his work.

He said, ⌒..'‿ ‿⊙⟼Oy. *It's ready.*

The best way to break into someone's house is not to go through the windows or the back door. That would look too suspicious and, while Wayfarer Dock was a relatively safe neighborhood, it still had a local organization, mighty fond of donuts and chai lattes, called the WDPD.

The best way to break into someone's house is to look like you weren't breaking in at all. Meep, having thought of all this already, opened Mr. Baz's front door and walked in with Pez and Laura.

"It's dark," said Meep.

"I'm trying to find the light," Pez said, feeling around the walls. Mr. Baz's walls were smooth as snakeskin and no matter how far Pez reached, he could not find so much as a nail, much less a light switch.

"Maybe while you're looking, you could find the thermostat too. It's so hot. What kind of person turns on their heat in the summer?" Meep shook her head. The dark was an uncomfortable thing but the dry heat that had replaced the ocean breeze turned it into an oppressive thing.

"Here," Laura said and clicked on her flashlight, fixing one problem. The narrow beam of light illuminated a bare hallway decorated by a single rug that had the words *Greetings* stamped in red.

"Shine the light over here," Meep said. "I think I see the thermostat." She was pointing at the wall down the hallway.

Laura passed the flashlight to Pez and followed behind him as he led the way toward Meep. From the back, Laura could see a sheen of sweat and the raised fine hairs on Pez's nape. "Don't worry," she said, quietly, "My nan says that nothing in the dark can hurt you."

"I'm not worried," said Pez.

Laura didn't disagree.

"Hurry up, I swear you two are slower than her chickens in the morning."

Pez winced at Meep's voice, which echoed uncomfortably in the empty hallway. "We're coming," he said. Then, they were at the end of the hall, and Pez was shining the flashlight onto the thermostat along with rows of pale cabinets, gleaming white marble countertops, and a stove, refrigerator, and sink.

"Meep," she said, "It's just an ordinary kitchen." She switched off the heat and turned on the AC, dialing it down to 60 degrees.

"Are you sure you should set it so low?" Pez said, "My mom and dad don't like it when I mess with the thermostat. Something about bills."

"Sometimes Pez—" Meep shook her head in deep disappointment. "I wonder if you're actually a kid. Bills? Really?"

"That's just what they say—"

"Hey guys, this kitchen is really clean, like *freakishly* clean." Laura wiped her finger across the countertop and held it up to show everyone. "It looks like it's never been used before."

Pez opened the refrigerator door. "You're right. There's also nothing in the fridge except a bag of cat food." He took it out and heaved it onto the counter. "You don't have to refrigerate cat food."

"Does he even have a cat?" Meep asked. But, before her friends could answer, a loud crackling came from further inside the house.

Now, normally if you heard a strange noise while you were in a strange person's house doing questionable things, you would most likely avoid said noise. Meep was not the kind of person to avoid strange noises, but rather the kind of person who was attracted to them. She raced toward the other room, followed closely by Pez and Laura. They ran past the stove and kitchen chairs, down the long hallway and into a space that could have been the living room if it housed a sofa and a TV set. At first, the three thought that their flashlight beam had turned red, but then blinked and realized that the red light was not coming from their flashlight.

It was coming from the floor.

As with any story, accounts differ, and the three had separate accounts of what happened next. For Meep, it was really quite simple. She heard a strange noise and saw a strange glow and needed a closer look. For Pez, it was the usual: trying to stop Meep from being Meep. For Laura, it was witnessing Meep step inside a painted pentagon on the floor and disappear with a crackling *pop*. All accounts had one thing in common though, and that was the last thing that they heard.

"Meep."

Mr. Baz was a man of routine. No, that's not quite right. He did have his routines, but he was not so much a man. Suffice to say, Mr. Baz was in the middle of said routine, predictably checking out his supplies when he saw, projected against the oblivious cashier's pale forehead, a small, red pentagon.

Like any sensible people, the In-Betweeners had reasoned that audible alarms were not practical in most situations and downright vexing in others. They made their alarms solely visual and tied them to both the owner and the things they watched. Mr. Baz's alarm was a miniature replica of his port—a perfect pentagon outlined in red.

Mr. Baz's jaw went slack. It was quite the sight for the poor cashier who had drawn two short straws—one for having to work on a Sunday and the other for being Mr. Baz's cashier. Her name was Georgia. She was Pez's older, more popular sister, but none of her years of experience as a seventeen-year-old, nor her job training, had prepared her for this afternoon, so she said the first thing that came to mind. "Paper or plastic?" The second thing that came to mind—*Oh my God, that's a lot of teeth*—went unsaid.

"Paper." Mr. Baz's jaw snapped shut. "And I'm paying with cash."

"Alrighty." Georgia checked him out, handed over his receipt and said, "Have a good day."

"Thank you," Mr. Baz said, then paused. "You have something on your forehead."

Georgia grabbed her phone from her back pocket and opened the camera app. She saw, to her horror, the largest pimple that ever pimpled, prominent in its place right in the center of her forehead. *Oh my God,* she thought, *I've turned into a unicorn! What am I going to do? Prom is next week!*

Mr. Baz left the store, secure in the knowledge that this incident would be forgotten in the wake of the cashier's new crisis.

Academics have long wondered if there are any universes beyond the known one, speculating on their potential existence and precise location if they did indeed exist. It would pain them to know that all their theories, despite being colorful, were wildly inaccurate, and it would pain them even more to know that the man who came the closest to the truth was a construction worker by the name of Carl Esteban Coldstrome—*very* distantly related to Laura and her mom, but not, as it turned out, to Mrs. Coldstrome.

He was deep in his cups, mourning a wife who had recently become his ex-wife, when he turned to his friend and said, "Hear me out, Tim. The universe and all other universes are a book."

Tim, ecstatic that Carl was no longer sobbing, nodded along enthusiastically.

"The three dimensions are the width, length, and height of the book." Carl took out his pocketbook, titled, *Compromise: The Key to Achieving a Lasting Marriage*, and slapped it on the counter to emphasize his point. The book had been a suggestion during his first counseling session and was, as far as Carl was concerned, just as useless as the counselor. His ex couldn't spell compromise if it bit her in the ass. "Our universe fits on one page in this book, but the other pages are made up of other universes. Then, there's time. That has to be the text on the page. Time crawls by slowly sometimes like the heaviest paragraphs, while other times it can skip along like dialogue."

Carl's analogy was mostly correct. It was missing one key element: the space between the pages. If he had any idea of the existence of the In-Between, he would have added, *hidden behind the text of time, and nestled in the interstitial space between the universal pages, is the In-Between.* Even Carl could not know the unknown unknowns, but eighty percent correct is still better than the academics.

The In-Betweeners were way ahead of Carl. Discovering the so-called book during the time of the Great Fear and, being conscious of the limits of their world, they had sought to expand its boundaries. Ports were just one of a few techniques used to do so. An average port could riffle through the pages of the book, enlarging or shrinking the space in the In-Between, but two particularly well-made and well-placed ports could act as a needle punching through the page. Anything could be dropped through the resultant hole from sound waves and objects to a girl called Meep.

Just as Pez and Laura were witnesses to Meep's sudden disappearance, Ms. Lam, Mr. Raz, and Mr. Maz were witnesses to her sudden reappearance in the In-Between with a sucking *pop.* They were just about to step into the port and make the journey themselves, so you can understand their utter surprise at seeing the girl.

For her part, Meep threw up. Going through a port was akin to partaking from an all-you-can-eat buffet and being dropped from a ninety-degree roller coaster. Meep's vomit sprayed over Mr. Raz's neat lines, obscuring the red in yellow bile and dispelling the glow. When there was nothing left in her stomach, Meep straightened and wiped the corners of her mouth. "*Ugh . . . What was that?*" She looked around, saw Ms. Lam, Mr. Raz, and Mr. Maz in all of their jaw-agape splendor, let out a startled *Meep*, and passed out. She missed the vomit, thankfully.

T⟶ ⟶◆'. ⟶◦⟶OO ◦ ℏ⟶◦◆, said Mr. Raz. *That wasn't supposed to happen.*

⟶⟶ℓ, ℏy O◦ ∩ ⟶ℓ⟶y •O. ⟶◦OO ℏ ��◦ℓ◦? *Fractals, why do I always get paired with imbeciles?* Ms. Lam's body shook in resignation from where she was sitting in the black sand.

TℏO◦O' ◆◦ℏ◦◆ ◦◆ ℏ ⟭y ⟶⟶ℏ. Tℏ◦ ◦ ◦◆ y◦, ⟶⟭. ⟶⟭. ◦'◦ ℏO ◦◆O ℏ◦ OO◦◆OO ℏ◦ ◦! *There's nothing wrong with my patch. This is on you, Ms. Lam. You're the one who designed this port!*

Ms. Lam stood and turned slowly toward Mr. Raz. At her full height, she towered over his thinner frame. ◦O y◦ ⟭ℓ⟶◦◆ ⟭O? *So you think?*

∩ ◦O⟶ℓℓy ℏ◦◆ ◦' ◆◦ ◦◆O' ⟶ℓ ◦O⟶ℓℓy. ∩ ⟭O⟶◆ ◦ ⟭⟶◆ ⟶◦ℓ ℏ◦◦•ℏ ⟶ ◦ ℏ◦◆ ⟭y⟭O ◦ℏO ℏ◦◆ ⟭⟶◆ ⟶◦ℓ ℏ◦◦•ℏ ◦◦? ∩ ⟭ ℏ⟶◦ ⟭OO◆ ◦◆ ℏO ◦•ℏ ◦ℓ⟶⟭O ⟶ ℏO ◦•ℏ ⟭O ◦ ⟶ ℏO ◦◆ ◦ℓ⟶⟭O ⟶ ℏO ◦◆ ⟭O. ◦ ◦

..ℏ↦.. ↦.. ..ℏ⊙ .⌐•ℏ.. ..⌐∓⊙ ↕↤.. ..ℏ⊙ .↦⌐•◆• ◁ℓ↦↕⊙ —Mr. Maz scratched his head— ↦.. ..ℏ⊙ .↦⌐•◆• ..⌐∓⊙ ↕↤.. ..ℏ⊙ .⌐•ℏ.. ◁ℓ↦↕⊙? ☐⌐. ◆⌐. .ℏ↦.. ∩ ∓⊙↦◆, .⊙↦ℓℓy ◆⌐ ⌐◆⊙'. ↦↦.ℓ... *I really think it's no one's fault really. I mean if we can travel through a port then maybe other things can travel through too? It must have been in the right place at the right time or at the wrong place at the wrong time. Or is that at the right time but the wrong place at the wrong time but the right place? You know what I mean, really no one's fault.*

∩ ⊙⌐•◆'. .⊙⊙ .ℏ↦↦.. y⌐. ∓⊙↦◆ ↦.. ↦ℓℓ, said Mr. Raz. Tℏ⌐. ◁⌐... ↦.. ↕⌐◆◆⊙↕...⊙⊙ .⌐ :.. ≑↦z'.. ¬⌐. ↕⌐.ℓ⊙ .ℏ⌐. ..ℏ⌐◆• ℏ↦.⊙ ↕⌐∓⊙ ..ℏ.⌐.•ℏ? *I don't see what you mean at all. This port was connected to Mr. Baz's. How could this thing have come through?*

:↦y↕⊙ ℏ⊙'. k⊙⊙◁⌐◆• ◁⊙...? Mr. Maz shrugged. ∩.. ⌐. .⊙↕.⊙..⌐◆• ↦ ℓ⌐.⌐⊙ ↦..⌐∓ ⌐... . ⌐◆. *Maybe he's keeping pets? It is secreting a liquid from its skin.* The In-Between had a climate with an average temperature of 305.3 Kelvin and very little fluctuation (with one notable exception) in their meteorological record. There were no seasons other than abominably hot, which was just fine for the In-Betweeners but not at all for visitors apparently.

Ms. Lam said, ˙.ℏ ◆⌐, ℏ⊙'. •⌐◆⊙ ◆↦..⌐⌐⊙ ℓ⌐⊙ λ.. ◁...⌐∓. ☐ℏ↦.. ⌐. ⌐. ↦↕⌐.. ..ℏ↦.. .⌐.ℓ⊙? *Oh no, he's gone native like Dr. Strom. What is it about that world?*

"Meep . . ." Meep mumbled in her unconsciousness.

∩.. .↦ℓ .! Mr. Maz said in alarm.

☐⊙ .ℏ⌐.ℓ⊙ ⌐⊙⊙◆..⌐y .ℏ⊙ .◁⊙↕⌐⊙., said Mr. Raz. ☐ℏ↦.. ⌐⌐ ⌐.'. ◁⌐⌐.⌐◆⌐..? Tℏ↦.. .⌐.ℓ⊙ ↕⌐ ⌐... ℓ⌐⊙ :.. ≑↦z, .↦ ⌐◆• ↕↦.⊙ ⌐↦ .ℏ⊙ ⌐◆⊙⊙⌐↕ℓ⊙. *We should identify the species. What if it's poisonous? That would be just like Mr. Baz, taking care of the inedible.*

Ms. Lam rubbed her thick fingers against her equally thick forehead. ⋒'Ŧ ——°_◆○○○ ⇕y ᶜ○ᶜ°…. *I'm surrounded by idiots.*

⋒ ○°◆'.. _○○ y°_ ⇕°◆…ᶜ⇕_°◆• ..° ..ℏ°_ ○°_⇕_—ᶜ°◆. Ⅱ↦_○ ..° ○◆ℓᶜ•ℏ..○◆ _. °◆ _ℏ↦.. y°_ ..ℏᶜ◆ ᶜ.. ᶜ_?

Engrossed in their debate, the In-Betweeners failed to notice that Meep was stirring. She rubbed her eyes, blinked groggily, and rubbed her eyes again. Ms. Lam's expansive back was facing her and, with the sand casting an iridescent sheen across her mottled hide, seemed like an oil slick attached to two thickset legs. Mr. Maz was partly hidden by Ms. Lam's shoulder, but from what Meep could see of his head, looked similar to an amalgamation of a frilled lizard and an eggplant. She almost missed Mr. Raz—his pale, svelte form the toothpick wedged between the molars of Mr. Maz and Ms. Lam.

Morphologically speaking, the In-Betweeners had little in common, yet they would classify themselves as a single species. For them, belonging to a species had nothing to do with the ability to interbreed and everything to do with what one ate. The In-Betweeners ate the same things—therefore they were the same species.

I'm dreaming, Meep thought. Her mom was fond of telling her that too many sweets before bedtime would give her terrible nightmares. It was one of the many things that her parents told her that she heard but didn't listen to, and she wondered if it had been the Skittles or the Twinkies this time. She watched as Mr. Maz swiped a long, black tongue across his eye. *Definitely, the Twinkies.* Her legs seemed to be working just fine in this dream though, and

Meep used them to get away from the In-Betweeners as fast as she could.

Mr. Baz had not asked to be an interdimensional explorer. He had been quite content to remain in the In-Between after they had managed to stabilize temperatures. He would have been a homebody forever if he had not had the fortune and misfortune of knowing Dr. Strom.

Dr. Strom was the missing link that joined the quintuple. She was Mr. Baz's closest friend, Ms. Lam's and Mr. Raz's co-conspirator, and Mr. Maz's mentor. Above all, Dr. Strom, with her prescient third eye, was a pioneer. During the Great Fear, when temperatures in the In-Between had dropped to an all time low of 288.7 K, she had been one of the first In-Betweeners to discover the unlimited travel potential of ports and had stepped through into another world. The In-Betweeners left behind, had received intermittent communications from Dr. Strom, but her last, enigmatic message: *They have climate-controlled dwellings!* had been sent years ago. The four, having become frustrated with her silence, had agreed that enough was enough and had decided to take the initiative and bring Dr. Strom home.

Initiative only went so far though. When it came to inter-dimensional travel, it was best to test the waters with the life of a single In-Betweener rather than four at once, and Mr. Baz had drawn the short straw. He had sketched out his own intricate port in blood, connected through the space between pages to a certain faded pentagon drawn on the living floor of a beachfront house, and stepped through his port to Wayfarer Dock a year ago.

The In-Between was a harsh, barren, interstitial space. There were few resources beyond iridescent black sand brimming from horizon to horizon, and little life beyond the few In-Betweeners who called this space home. As such, the In-Betweeners had become a self-reliant lot. Rather than, *when life gives you lemons, make lemonade*, the In-Betweeners would say, *when life doesn't give you lemons, make lemonade from your blood.*

You can imagine then that Wayfarer Dock had come as quite a pleasant shock to Mr. Baz. Neatly lined homes built from a glut of materials lined a paved road. No shimmering sand existed except the beige grains washed onto the beach by water as far as his eyes could see. Not drinkable (Mr. Baz had found out the hard way) but that was what the tap was for, he supposed. Anything that wasn't supplied by the beachfront house could be found in what the locals called "stores." No more waiting months for a mogre to grow on his hide; he could simply walk into the "grocery store" and pick up a bag of cat food and consume kibble in the handfuls. No more opening up a vein to draw their ports—a task that could take months as the In-Betweeners took caution not to draw too much blood; he could simply stroll into a "hardware store" and buy a can of red paint. And the best part and the part that really sold Wayfarer Dock to him, was HVAC. Outdoor temperatures may have been chilly, but that hardly mattered when he could return to his climate-controlled dwelling and his beloved thermostat, set at a balmy temperature of 95 degrees (Fahrenheit, not Kelvin). The terror of the Great Fear was truly a thing of the past. Mr. Baz had found paradise.

The language had been a challenge to learn at first, but once he realized that it had few rigid rules (similar to port design), he focused on rote memorization and was fluent in no time. With a trench coat to cover his pronounced hunch back, Mr. Baz thought that he had assimilated quite well to this new world of his. The only thing left was to bring over the other In-Betweeners and locate his wayward friend. It should have been simple . . . and it would have been if not for those meddling children.

Shortly after Meep's disappearance, Pez found himself panicking. He was the group's fixer, the restraining hand of order to Meep's chaos, but for the first time in his short life, he had no idea what to do. "She-she-she's gone!" Pez stuttered. "Vanished! Poof! Disappeared! She—"

"Disintegrated," Laura supplied helpfully.

Pez moaned. "What are we going to do? Where did she go? Is she gone gone? She can't be gone gone . . . How are we going to get her back? How do we explain this to our parents?"

While Pez was going through a mix of emotions, Laura knelt down and examined the pentagon. She saw the five candelabra candlesticks or, more accurately, five nubs sticking out of pools of wax, and reached out to touch a faded red line.

Pez grabbed her shoulder. "Don't touch that! You don't know what it's going to do!"

Laura stood and turned to face Pez. "I think we should talk to my nan."

"I know you think Mrs. Coldstrome has all the answers, but I don't think she's going to have an answer for this."

"She will," Laura said with all of the assurance of an eleven-year-old and grabbed Pez's hand, tugging him toward the front door.

"Laura, wait—" Pez pulled his hand back. "We have to put

everything back where we found it. The last thing we need is for Mr. Baz to know we were here."

Ignoring him, Laura continued on toward the door and opened it, coming face to face with a startled Mr. Baz. "Too late."

In his rush to return, Mr. Baz had lost his usual trench coat and there was nothing to distract Laura and Pez from seeing all of his In-Between splendor.

Laura stared at him, blinking slowly. "You're different."

"Laura, what's going on?" Pez pushed to her side and, seeing Mr. Baz, let out a girlish scream. "Gah! It's a monster!"

"Monster?" Mr. Baz muttered under his breath. "Really? There's nothing monstrous about me. I'm Mr. Baz, and you two must be the ones who triggered my alarm."

"*You're* Mr. Baz?" Pez sputtered. "*The* Mr. Baz?"

"The one and only." Mr. Baz bowed.

"The Mr. Baz that everyone says is a Russian spy? The Mr. Baz that everyone thinks has a serious skin condition or is an albino?" Pez asked.

"Is that what they say about me?" Mr. Baz was not sure whether he should feel insulted by his neighbors' highly inaccurate assumptions or tickled that they even thought of him to begin with. "And who are you two?"

"I'm Laura." Laura grabbed Mr. Baz's clawed hand in her small one and shook it vigorously. "Pleased to meet you. That one is Jordan, but everyone calls him Pez."

Pez's voice was strained when he said, "*Laura*, don't tell him our names."

"Why not? I think we could be good friends, and he might be able to tell us where Meep went."

"Meep? There are three of you?" Mr. Baz asked with a sinking sense of dread.

"Angelique, but we all call her Meep on account of the sound she makes," said Laura. "She's our friend and disappeared through the badly drawn thingy you have in your living room."

"The port?"

Laura snapped her fingers. "That's what my nan called them. Yep, the port."

Mr. Baz blinked at her slowly. "I think I should meet your nan."

"I *told* you Pez," said Laura.

Meep had been walking for what she thought was hours, but in reality was probably more like thirty minutes. She was sweaty, tired, sore, and desperately thirsty. And she was a hundred percent over this dream. "Wake up," she muttered, closed her eyes, and pinched herself. Like the previous nineteen times, pinching did nothing but add to the red on her arm. Meep did not open her eyes to a soft bed, sheets on the ground, kicked to the floor overnight. She did not wake up from Pez's shaking, or even to the dreaded S word from her mom. *Angelique, it's time for school.* When she opened her eyes, the only thing she was greeted by was black sand.

"THIS SUCKS!" Meep screamed and kicked at the sand. "MEEEEEEP. IHATETHISIHATETHISIHATETHISIHA-TETHISIHATETHISIHATETHISIHATETHIS." Meep collapsed onto the sand and rolled flat on her back. "Worst. Dream. Ever."

She wondered what Pez and Laura would do. Ever the boring

rule-follower, Pez would probably try to reason himself out of this situation. Meep could hear his voice now. *Did you try pinching yourself? I hear that always works.* Not helpful. Meep rarely listened to Pez, and she didn't think that now was the time to start.

Laura, then? She had always been the odd one in their trio. Meep and Pez had known each other since they were toddlers, but Laura was a new addition to their group. Laura was *different* (Meep had used another word, but her mom had insisted that "different" was better), taking everything literally and interjecting with her random, Laura-ness comments. Though sometimes, Meep had to admit, she had an uncanny way of being right.

What would Laura say? She would say, Meep thought with a growing disquiet, *this isn't a dream.* She would also say, *There's something poking you in the back.*

Meep flipped over onto her stomach and dug through the sand until she found the object. If she didn't know better, she'd think the cone-shaped shell that fit perfectly in the palm of her hand was a barnacle. She didn't know better as mogres were not at all related to barnacles and had nothing in common with those marine crustaceans except for their protective calcareous (siliceous, in the case of mogres) carapaces, or their soft cores, or a tendency to be hermaphroditic. Really, barnacles and mogres had very little in common.

Meep pinched the mogre between her fingers and nearly let out another startled *Meep* as a two inch spike protracted from the shell. The spike was an adaptation that allowed the organism to attach itself to the hides of In-Betweeners. Seeing as there were few other resources found in the In-Between, mogres and In-Betweeners had developed a special relationship, each treating the other as food.

Meep got to her feet again, slipped the mogre into her pocket, and continued walking. It wasn't like there was anything else to do in this dream.

She had been walking for actual hours this time and had seen nothing but black sand, so it was understandable that her first glimpse of water was met by confusion. The water was not found in a large body such as the sea that Meep was used to in Wayfarer Dock, or even in a small body like the puddles that she took a perverse joy in splashing through every spring. It was found in a huge gelatinous sack. Meep approached it, looked up at the rainbow of refracted light, and poked it. It jiggled, like gelatinous sacks of liquid tend to do, and felt slimy to the touch.

"Ewwww . . . that's disgusting!" Meep exaggerated wiping her finger on her pants. She was about to go into histrionics over the grossness of the sack, but then, realizing that she had no audience, she sat back to look at the sack instead.

Meep, she thought and silently congratulated herself. Her imagination was going into overdrive tonight. Meep was parched in her dream, and her imagination had conjured up water. Not in the form that ordinary people would dream of water, but in a giant, gelatinous sack. *You just can't make this stuff up,* Meep thought and vowed to abstain from Twinkies from now on.

Next to the sack, Meep was just beginning to notice, was another port. This one was much larger than the one she had run from hours ago. A thick, glowing red circle was delineated in the sand, a dense design of coils twisted around cylinders filling the space inside. Unlike the other port, this one was giving off a lot of heat.

Unbeknownst to Meep, the two objects were known as ⌒◆ .. and ⌒◆ ..ℏ, liberally translated to *The Furnace* and *The Cooler*, and they were, inarguably, the pillars that supported the lives of the In-Betweeners.

The Furnace was the In-Betweeners' solution to the Great Fear. When temperatures began dropping precipitously, the In-Betweeners had been compelled to act. As a cold blooded species, the In-Betweeners thrived in temperatures higher than 302.6 K. While they could survive for a short time in colder temperatures, their metabolisms could not function effectively. If left too long in the cold, an In-Betweener's body would start to arrest, all motion stopping completely as they entered a state of hibernation. To prevent this, the pioneers of their species had come together to create The Furnace, an augmented port that permanently linked the In-Between to another gaseous dimension and utilized its calefaction to stabilize their own temperatures.

The Cooler was the only source of freshwater in the In-Between. It had been compiled through a painstaking network of numerous linked ports throughout the In-Between to consolidate their limited sources of water in one spot. The In-Betweeners did not need much to quench their thirst, but all life needed water. When they did, they would port themselves to The Cooler, unhinge their jaws, and pierce The Cooler with rows of needle-like teeth. After assuaging their thirst, the In-Betweeners repaired the holes left behind with saliva, not wasting a drop. It was neat and easy like a lamprey feeding on the bodily fluids of another fish.

You might be wondering why the In-Betweeners decided to place the two things critical to their survival together. For security, of course.

None of that mattered to Meep who was simply, desperately thirsty. Unfortunately, her blunted teeth were more suited to masticating candy than piercing The Cooler. She tried poking the sack again, but her nails were also not sharp enough to break through the gelatinous coating. *What was the point of dreaming up water when you couldn't drink it?* Meep stared at The Cooler, biting her lip in frustration.

The idea came to her slowly. She reached into her pocket to take out the mogre. Sticking the mogre to The Cooler at eye-level, she pinched it and watched as the two inch spike shot out and pierced the sack. She removed the mogre, a thin trickle of water streaming out of the resulting hole. *I really am a genius*, Meep thought as she positioned her mouth below the stream. *Gross, it's lukewarm. I need to dream up some ice water next time.*

As Meep was washing her face and hands, she failed to notice that the pressure of the water was making the hole larger. What had once been a trickle was now more like a gush, expanding by the second. The stream of water puddled at Meep's feet and flowed toward The Furnace. When the water touched the glowing red lines, it sizzled, and The Furnace began to flicker.

If Meep had been with the In-Betweeners, they might have been able to save The Furnace, averting disaster before it was too late. Unfortunately for everyone involved, Meep was alone and oblivious to the ramification of her actions. Maybe if she had known, she would have done something, but with Meep, you never knew.

The Furnace flickered one last, protesting time before being washed away.

After Pez had gotten over his initial shock and Laura had caught Mr. Baz up on the details of Meep's disappearance, Mr. Baz surmised that Meep had most likely been ported through to the In-Between. Mr. Baz then tried to reestablish his port with a fresh coat of red paint and new candlesticks, but it was all to no avail. The port refused to cooperate—unknown to Mr. Baz, this was most likely due to an earlier vomiting incident—and could not even establish a link strong enough to send a message to the In-Between.

While he had been listening to Laura talk about her grandmother, Mr. Baz felt a growing suspicion. Surely, they had not been this close to each other this whole time. Seeing as the port was a bust, Mr. Baz thought that the next best thing was to confirm his suspicion. The three left his home and walked down the street to Mrs. Coldstrome's house.

Laura was the first to knock on the door. "Nan, it's me! I've got a friend you should meet!"

"Hold on a second dear. I'm putting on my wig." Mrs. Coldstrome's muffled voice could be heard through the door. When she opened it a minute later, she took one look at Mr. Baz standing next to her granddaughter and sighed. "Oh dear, I think there's a story here."

"It is you," said Mr. Baz.

Mrs. Coldstrome was short in stature, but she wore a towering chartreuse wig that added at least a foot to her height. It was difficult to focus on her face with that eyesore of a wig (which was just the way Mrs. Coldstrome preferred it). Laura rarely saw her grandmother without the wig, and never in front of strangers, so she watched in surprise as her grandmother took it off.

"Um . . . Laura, your grandma has a third eye," said Pez.

"Yep, and?" said Laura. She was puzzled by Pez's behavior. He didn't usually point out the obvious.

Pez blinked. "Did you know your grandma has a third eye?"

"Of course. Doesn't your grandma have three eyes?" asked Laura.

"No." Pez shook his head slowly. "No, she doesn't."

"Huh, how boring," said Laura.

"I think you should all come inside. It looks like I have some explaining to do," Mrs. Coldstrome said. She led them into her well-furnished home and gestured to the living room sofa set that had just been purchased from the newest IKEA catalogue. "Sit. I'm going to make us some refreshments."

Not knowing what else to do, the three sat down together on the largest couch, with Laura in the middle, Pez on her left, and Mr. Baz on her right. They watched as Mrs. Coldstrome came out with a tray that had two glasses of milk, a plate of cookies, and a carton of eggs on it. She placed the tray on the coffee table in front of the three and said to Laura, "I made the chocolate cookies you like dear." To Mr. Baz, she said, "Have you tried the chicken eggs in this world? They are even better than the cat food."

"Thanks, Nan," said Laura. She grabbed a cookie from the tray and almost dropped it at Pez's hard nudge. "What?"

"*Don't eat that!*" Pez whispered.

"Why not?" Laura asked. "We've had my nan's cookies before."

Pez looked pointedly at Mrs. Coldstrome and Mr. Baz. He was a polite twelve-year-old boy, and at the moment, his sense of alarm was struggling with his sense of decorum.

"He just needs some time to adjust," Mrs. Coldstrome said,

"You grew up with me and are familiar with my eccentricities. This is still new to Pez."

Mr. Baz opened up the carton, took out a speckled brown egg with two of his clawed fingers and held it up to his eye. "Have you been here this entire time, Dr. Strom?" he asked while examining the egg.

"Yes, for the most part. It's a long story," said Mrs. Coldstrome.

"We don't have anywhere else to be, and you owe it to me after all this time," Mr. Baz said.

Mrs. Coldstrome did not disagree, and so, she shared her own adventures in Wayfarer Dock and In-Between. Back when she had been known as Dr. Strom to her peers, she had stumbled upon this world purely by accident when her port had connected with a humans' poorly drawn symbol. The human, Amelia ("That's my mom!" Laura interjected), had decided to paint a red pentagram on her bedroom floor in what Dr. Strom later learned was her goth phase. The pentagram was a useless shape, but the *pentagon* inside the pentagram . . . well, that had been enough to establish an ephemeral link with Dr. Strom's port. Instead of going to the Tartarian Pits, Dr. Strom had stepped through her port to end up in a teenager's bedroom.

Her appearance had been quite a shock to Amelia at first, but the two had quickly become friends and, upon learning that Dr. Strom needed hotter temperatures to thrive, Amelia had taken the Dr. to her parents' empty beachfront property in Wayfarer Dock and introduced her to the wonderful thermostat. It had been Amelia's idea to use a wig to hide Dr. Strom's third eye, though the color had been entirely Dr. Strom's idea as it matched her eye. The wig allowed her to blend in with the locals and go outside without causing a commotion. When Amelia's parents had passed away two years later, Dr. Strom had taken on the role of Amelia's "aunt," sparing her from the foster system, formally adopting her, and becoming Mrs. Coldstrome. There was much more to her story, but there were not enough cookies or eggs on the tray to accommodate every single detail.

"I decided to stay," Mrs. Coldstrome finished.

"To think you've been here this whole time, right under my nose, and I never knew it." said Mr. Baz.

"Don't be too hard on yourself. When I first arrived in Wayfarer Dock, I didn't dare set foot outside for the longest time. Your mother—" Mrs. Coldstrome nodded toward Laura, "—was the sweetest and made regular cat food trips for me. She also introduced me to the exquisiteness of a freshly laid egg. Speaking of which, Mr. Baz, you should eat that one you've been glaring at. I promise it won't bite."

Shrugging, Mr. Baz unhinged his jaw and popped the egg inside. His jaw snapped closed, *crunch*, and his eyes closed in bliss. "Mmm."

Pez watched Mr. Baz eat, his eyes wide. "*Fuck.*"

Laura nudged Pez in the side. "Language."

"I understand the appeal of this world, Dr. Strom—" said Mr. Baz.

"I'd prefer if you called me Mrs. Coldstrome. I haven't been Dr. Strom for a long time."

"Fine, Mrs. Coldstrome. Climate-controlled dwellings are an assurance that is hard to pass, but could you not have sent us a message? We would have understood."

"I thought that you didn't need me anymore. The Great Fear

had come to an end, and the In-Between was secure."

"She also had me to take care of!" Laura added.

"That's very kind my dear. You were never hard to raise," said Mrs. Coldstrome. "I left a port behind in the beach house on the off chance that you would need to leave the In-Between. Isn't that how you ended up here?"

"I did come through about a year ago and was in regular communication with Ms. Lam, Mr. Raz, and Mr. Maz, when those two happened," said Mr. Baz ruefully, pointing at Laura and Pez. His finger faltered when he saw the two bright red miniature circles projected on their foreheads.

⋂◆ „, Mr. Baz and Mrs. Coldstrome cursed together.

Mr. Baz and Mrs. Coldstrome were not the only In-Betweeners to see the alarm. For a port as important as The Furnace, the In-Betweeners had ensured that the attached alarm would be noticeable, if not loud. At the exact moment when the water hit The Furnace, every In-Betweener across the In-Between and beyond saw the same thing: a bright red circle projected across a forehead or a hand (if foreheads were not available). It was almost redundant as temperatures immediately began to drop, and all of the In-Betweeners headed toward The Furnace as if their world was ending. Since it was, they were moving quite quickly.

Ms. Lam, Mr. Raz, and Mr. Maz were the closest to Meep and therefore were the first to reach her.

⌐⊢↦⇕⌐↦ℓ⌐ ⌐ℏ↦⌐⋅ ℏ↦→⌐ ⌐ ○∘◆⊙? cried Ms. Lam.

"Umm . . . Hi!" Meep waved cheerily. She was no longer afraid of the In-Betweeners and their alien forms. This was a dream, and

Meep had the invincibility of a dreamer.

Th⊙ ⊥.◆⊢↥⇕⊙ ⚬ •⚬◆⊙, Mr. Raz said in disbelief. ≙◆⊙ ℏ⊢. ℏ⊢≺≺⊙◆⊙⊙ .⚬ ⚬ ⊥⊢.⊙.? λ⚬⊙ ⚬ ⇕⚬◆⊤⊙ ⊙⊙y.ℏ⚬◆•? The Cooler, which had been full before Meep, now resembled a deflating balloon. Water continued to leak out, at a much slower rate, soaking into the sand.

□⊙'⊙ ⊙⚬⊤⊙⊙! λ⊢⊤◆⊙⊙! λ⚬◆⊙! λ⊙⚬y⊙⊙! ∩ ⇕⊢◆ ⊢ℓ⊙⊢⊙y ⊱⊙⊙ℓ ⚬ •⊙⚬◆• ⇕⚬ℓ⊙, Mr. Maz said. *We're doomed! Damned! Done! Destroyed! I can already feel it getting cold*

"I don't know what you're saying," Meep said. Honestly, why did the monsters in her dream insist on speaking a language she couldn't understand? Weren't you supposed to understand everything in your own dream?

∩. ⊙⚬⊙ ◆⚬. ⊙◆⊙⊙⊢◆⊙ ⊸, said Mr. Raz. ⊀⊙⊤⊙⊤⇕⊙ ℏ⊢. ⫶. ≙⊢z.⚬ℓ⊙ ⊸? Th⊙y ⊙⚬ ◆⚬. ≺⊙⊢ ⚬◆ ⚬◆•⊙ ⊢◆⊙ ⊙.⚬≺⚬◆⊙ ⇕⊙ ⚬◆ English. ⊀⊙⇕⊢ℓℓ ⚬ ℓ⊙⚬◆•., ⫶. ⸱⊢⊤⊢◆⊙ ⫶. ⫶⊢z. *It does not understand us. Remember what Mr. Baz told us? They do not speak in tongues and respond best in English. Recall our lessons, Ms. Lam and Mr. Maz.*

Meep, hearing one word that she recognized, brightened. "Do- you- speak- En-glish?"

Ms. Lam's dark eyes stared at Meep. "You are evil."

"Excuse me?"

"An evil, evil pet," Ms. Lam continued. ∩◆ ∩◆ ∩◆ ∩◆ ⸱ Ms. Lam was just beginning to learn English, and she was feeling quite a few emotions at the moment. There are just some things that the English language cannot convey, so we'll leave them in their original text.

"You've done a terrible thing, girl," Mr. Raz explained. "Our Furnace is gone, and we need it to stay warm. The blood of a hundred of In-Betweeners went into The Furnace. They are gone now, like their work, and with it, our future."

"Meep, all I did was try to get a drink."

ƛ°○ y○_ ○→°◆ _ħ⊙ _ħ°ℓ⊙ ⊔°°ℓ⊙_ .°°? Mr. Maz had never been able to master the English language. His listening comprehension was superb, but he found that his thick tongue just could not handle English's delicate consonants and vowels.

"Huh?" said Meep.

"My colleague wants to know if you took all of our water as well," Mr. Raz said.

"I only drank a little bit. The rest of it spilled out onto that circle-thingy. Whose bright idea was it to put them next to each other?"

For once, the In-Betweeners were speechless.

"It's too hot here anyway. If you ask me, I did you all a favor." Meep crossed her arms.

ƛ°°∓○○! cried Mr. Maz.

"Since you've destroyed all hope for life in the In-Between, our only option now is to escape to your world. I wonder what your world is like, but first, the most important question: what is the average temperature?" asked Mr. Raz.

"We have different seasons. I'd say the average annual temperature is 66 degrees Fahrenheit," Meep said.

"Fahrenheit? Is that 305 Kelvin?" said Ms. Lam.

Meep, who had no idea what Kelvin was, shrugged. "Sure."

"It's settled then. We're going to your world since you've

destroyed ours," said Ms. Lam.

"Ooo field trip." Meep jumped and clapped gleefully.

Ms. Lam had been the one to design the port that had brought Meep to the In-Between, and so felt that it was her duty to supervise the making of this port, arguably the most important port of their lives, lest Mr. Maz and Mr. Raz bungle it again. "Don't just sit there. Let's get started. The rest of the In-Betweeners are coming, and we're going to need a big one."

In the heat and gloom of a little beachfront house in Wayfarer Dock, a pentagon began to glow.

A lot of strange people lived in Wayfarer Dock (if you wanted to be precise, you could say that exactly a hundred-and-three strange people lived in Wayfarer Dock). Most of them could be found in the wonderful new retirement community that, to the locals, seemed to have sprung up overnight. However, the strangest by far were three children by the names of Meep, Pez, and Laura.

One could argue that all children are peculiar in their own ways, but these three weren't peculiar in the sense of chasing after ladybugs (the redder, the better) for a snack, or keeping a collection of tarantulas (twenty-nine of which were native to North America) pinned in glass displays around their room, they were peculiar in the sense of their experiences and responsibilities. Gone were the days of being egg thieves, Meep had become an inter-dimensional traveler and the perpetrator of a second Great Fear (all in one night), while the three had overseen the mass migration of an entire species of In-Betweeners. They were culture bridgers, interpreters of tongues, and cat food suppliers when all of the local stores were sold out.

And they were, from the point of view of the In-Betweeners, most importantly, the newest members of the family.

CASTLE RULES

Sandra Unerman

Sir Drumlin Moore and his wife Cassiopeia quarrelled on the day after they returned from their honeymoon, on the eighteenth of June 1931. That morning, Cass welcomed Drumlin's offer to show her his favourite room in her new home. She had seen little of the castle before the wedding, since their courtship had been brief, although delightful. Both had lost their parents when they were young and were used to relying on their own judgement. They had seen no sense in a long engagement.

Most of the castle was old-fashioned and a touch dilapidated. Cass looked forward to redecorating but not until she had a thorough grasp of her husband's taste. Now he took her to a wide room with a painted ceiling of snakes and ladders. A chess game was set out on a table in one corner and Mah-jong tiles on another opposite. In the centre stood an enormous drum, with a deck of cards spread out on top. Everything here was in pristine condition.

53

"This is where the games start," Drumlin said.

Cass walked towards the chess set. The pieces were made of gold and silver, in sixteenth century costumes, with eyes of emerald or ruby. "These are splendid. Who is your opponent?"

"You, I hope. When I've taught you the rules."

"I already know them." Cass allowed herself to be a touch offended. "We played chess the second time we met, remember, after the Hunt Ball at Lady Elizabeth's."

"Not my version," he said. "The old games are not complicated enough for me. I've invented new rules to make them more fun."

"Good." Cass nodded, slowly. "The more rules, the more scope to break them."

"Not in my games. You'll land in trouble, if you break my rules."

He was serious. Cass ought to have let the moment go but she could not resist saying, "Only if I'm found out."

He glowered at her, head bent, mouth pressed down as he worked his jaw back and forth. She was amused, not for the first time, by the way his sulks spoiled his good looks.

"I won't have that," he said. "You must stick to the rules."

She was still amused, enamoured as ever of his springy dark curls, his thin, sharp face and elegant body. But she would not be bullied. "Nonsense," she said. "We can have much more fun my way."

"I thought you would understand." His scowl did not lighten. "You enjoy chess and bridge. I thought you'd appreciate my variations."

"Of course. I'm looking forward to learning them. Just be ready for me to test your wits by cheating, when I can."

"That doesn't work," he said. "If that's your attitude, you'll have to be formally bound to obey the rules or I won't let you play."

"Bound?"

"I've invested in a spell from the Royal Thaumaturgical Society, one that holds people to their word or the consequences are unpleasant."

"You've done what?" Spells from that source were reputed to be fabulously expensive, as well as more reliable than most, and Cass knew enough to realise that unpleasant meant painful, if not life threatening. "What possessed you to do anything so ridiculous?"

"I didn't expect to use it on you." But he didn't sound repentant. "I just needed a fall back, in case I'm challenged by someone I can't trust."

"Why didn't you tell me any of this before?"

"I wanted to surprise you, introduce you to the fun we can have here all at once."

"Then you should give me a chance to show how much fun we can have, if we do things my way."

"No," Drumlin said. He turned and strode from the room, so fast that Cass would have had to run to catch up. She waited for a few moments but he did not return. So she went to make friends with the housekeeper and the cook, necessary tasks which she had intended to put off until later.

She did not see Drumlin again until the cocktail hour. He came into the drawing room, just as she was wondering whether to mix her own drink. Twigs were caught in his hair and his shoes were muddy. He must have been out in the woods to walk off his temper. He prepared her usual Manhattan and handed it to her in silence.

She smiled her thanks and said, "Do you want a bath? We can have dinner put back?"

Drumlin studied her. She had dressed carefully for the evening, not too grandly, since they were alone, but in the cream silk trouser set from Paris, which flattered her tanned skin and shiny, conker hair. She wore the pearl necklace and earrings Drumlin had given her. For the first time, his glance did not show his appreciation of her appearance.

"Never mind dinner," he said. "Not until you've agreed to be bound."

"Don't be absurd." Cass was hungry and disappointed by the day. "You're beginning to sound as though you only married me for the sake of your games."

"Almost." He downed half his drink in a gulp. "I've nearly fallen for other pretty girls, you know, but none of them enjoyed games the way you do." He might have been talking about a doll he had picked out from a row.

"You never told me that," she said, in her sweetest voice, to hide her resentment.

His smile was brief. "You fell for me too, didn't you? We've had fun together, so far."

"Darling!" Angrier still, Cass raised her glass in a grudging admission.

He toasted her in return and refilled both glasses. "There you are then. Just take the oath and we're all set."

"Set for what?" Cass stood up. "Why should we do everything your way?"

He blinked. "Because you're my wife."

"That doesn't make you Scheherazade's Sultan. Do you mean to choose my friends? Or the way I spend my money?"

"No, no. Just what's really important."

"And what about what's important to me? Like breaking rules, if I choose, without being strangled by my own jewellery or whatever gruesome penalty your oath exacts."

"I'll excuse you the oath, if you give me your promise. I'll trust you."

"I'll already have lost the game that matters to me, won't I, if I do that?"

"You've won me and your position as my wife. Isn't that enough for you?"

Cass set her glass down gently, so as not to throw it in his face. "You should have asked me that, before you proposed."

"I thought you loved me. I won't have anyone in the castle who spoils my games."

"Take care, then." Cass did not lose her temper as often as Drumlin but when she did, the results could be overwhelming. She walked to the door and looked back. His appearance was as dashing as ever but everything she had desired in him was turned to ash. The castle was a dungeon, his friends were bores and the prospect of his kisses repellent. "I may weasel a way back inside when you least expect to see me."

Cass drove back to town that evening in the little white roadster given to her by Drumlin, although she left the pearls behind, along with all the other presents. She had chosen the car herself and counted it a small compensation for the destruction of her hopes. Drumlin did not come after her and she made no attempt to contact him, except in response to the letters from his solicitors. He did not suggest a divorce, which suited her, since it would prevent her from making the same mistake with someone else. She turned down the allowance he offered, on account of the money she had inherited from the grandmother who had brought her up. She was not wealthy, by Drumlin's standards, but reasonably comfortable.

She preferred the company of the friends who teased her, to those who tried to commiserate. Before long, both sorts forgot her troubles and she settled down to the life she had led before she met Drumlin. But she was restless. Her London seemed full of divorced wives, who ran interior design businesses or embarked on archaeological expeditions. Cass had no desire to express herself so strenuously but she missed the sense of purpose which had once kept her busy, in search of love and romance. She wanted something new to stretch her mind and test her will.

Her career as a plumber began by accident. Irritated by the mess made when a workman sorted out a leaking tap in her flat, she decided she could have done a better job herself. The excellent plumber who had been responsible for maintenance of the building where she lived had not long retired. Cass persuaded him to give her lessons and proved her skill over the stopped sink at the house of her friend Rosalie. As she began to accept work from strangers, Cass worried that she ought not to compete with men who needed the wages. But women on their own would rather have her in their houses and she enjoyed putting things right for them. Out on a job, she dressed in overalls, with her hair tucked into a cap, so that passers-by sometimes mistook her for a man.

Meanwhile, Drumlin held parties at the castle, which soon became famous. Cass learned about them from the newspapers as well as their mutual friends. The guests were the cream of society, with a mixture of aristocrats, distinguished scholars and actors. They were invited for weekends, at which they tested their skills against one another, until the best were challenged by their host, The prizes, if anyone beat him, were supposed to be magnificent, although Cass was sceptical of the gush in the papers about authentic flying carpets and tame leopards with jewelled collars. Drumlin had never displayed that kind of vulgarity to her.

The reports irritated her, for reasons she admitted only to herself. Drumlin had turned her life upside down, however well she had recovered. She begrudged how little her departure appeared to have affected him. All the same, she had no intention of interfering, until Rosalie was refused admittance to the castle.

Rosalie went as the guest of a young aviator, a last-minute substitute for a cousin who was unwell. But when she gave her name at the door, the butler had been apologetic. "I'm sorry, Miss, I can't let you in. You're on my list."

The aviator had made enough fuss to earn them both an interview with Drumlin. He had been courteous but unrepentant. "I won't ask you to keep secrets from Cassiopeia. You're too close a friend of hers. It's better if you don't come in at all."

Cass had been fascinated, as well as provoked. "What is he so determined to hide?"

Rosalie shrugged. "He's convinced you mean to gate-crash one of his weekends in disguise, to ruin his games. He reckons the less you find out the better."

Cass's eyes widened. She had almost forgotten the threat she had made, when she walked out on Drumlin. "I didn't realise."

Rosalie misunderstood. "Never mind, my dear, you're worth ten of him, even if it was embarrassing to be turned away like a bankrupt gambler."

"Embarrassing and unfair. Besides, if that's what he thinks, I'd hate to disappoint him."

Cass studied the newspapers and gleaned hints from people who could not resist mentioning their experiences, even while they refused to go into the details. The weekenders she knew were also reluctant to talk, maybe from fear they would lose favour with Drumlin and maybe from reluctance to discuss their own embarrassments. No betting was allowed in the castle, according to the newspaper reports. But for the wilder games, Drumlin would arrange a forfeit, a swim in January or a childhood terror to be confronted. Not everyone was ready to be laughed at afterwards.

Her first attempt to gate-crash was arranged through Rosalie's aviator friend. He used his flying club acquaintances to start a rumour about a chess prodigy on a visit to London, a young woman from Boston in the States. She was supposed to have beaten a dozen grand masters at her home but was too shy to take part in public competitions.

When the invitation to the castle arrived, Cass invested in a severe navy suit and a wig of dark curls, crimped and rigid. At the door, the butler, new since her day, greeted her politely, studied her invitation and asked her to wait. She guessed at her failure, even before a grey-haired stranger came forth to inspect her. "My apologies, ma'am," he said. "I don't recall your name. I come from Boston and I've played chess there since I was six years old."

Cass had practised her American accent but now she did not

bother to argue. She smiled, mostly at the butler. "Another time," she said and walked away.

Her next attempt went no better. A plumbing job introduced her to a woman, whose daughter was ladies' maid to one of Drumlin's regular guests. For a consideration, the maid was persuaded to feign illness and offer Cass as a last-minute substitute. But at the servants' entrance, the housekeeper said, "Haven't you brought your papers?"

"I beg your pardon?" Cass kept her eyes down and her voice meek. If she behaved like a servant, with luck, the housekeeper would not recognise her in her maid's outfit.

"We never admit servants unless they've been in post for twelve months or have references from previous appointments."

Cass tried to look shocked. "But what will my mistress do without me?"

"One of our staff will help her," the housekeeper said. "You may have a lift to the railway station in half an hour."

Cass brooded for months after that, before it occurred to her to try a simpler, bolder trick. She waited until the Sunday of one of the most lavish parties, according to the papers. Mid-morning, she turned up at the kitchen door, in her plumber's gear, walking as much like a man as she could. "Blockage in the conservatory pipes," she said in her deepest voice and strode in. "Will you show me down to the undersides?"

One of the kitchen maids took her down. Cass stopped at the nearest tangle of pipes. "I'd better check these first."

They were in a sort of passage, dark and grubby. "I've work to do upstairs," the kitchen maid said. "Can you find your way back on your own?"

"Off you go." Cass did not look round. "Don't worry about me."

Once she was alone, she delved into the bottom layer of her tool box. There she had packed a man's fawn blazer and a silk tie. The shirt and trousers she already wore under her overalls. She took off her cap and tidied her wig, wheaten blond this time, short and floppy. A few moments later, she climbed the stairs and strolled out into a back corridor.

The castle had been redecorated. The drawing room was white and gold, with pale, sleek sofas and glass-topped tables. Cass wondered if a woman had helped Drumlin with the designs and if she was also responsible for the flower arrangements, asymmetric clusters of roses and thistles. His female relatives were too old and staid to have devised anything so stylish.

The crowd in that room and others were well-groomed and cheerful, their clothes just on the smart side of casual. Cass spotted a few acquaintances but nobody likely to see through her disguise, provided she sustained her masculine slouch and darkened her voice. She overheard accents from the United States, from France and maybe Italy. Intense political arguments tangled with chatter about cricket and the best routes to motor out of London.

The games were spread all over the place, with onlookers at many of them. Cass watched an unrecognisable card game in the library, a version of indoor croquet in the hall, and a silent blind man's bluff up and down the stairs. Her neck itched as she waited for Drumlin to loom up behind her. He never appeared and eventually, in the morning room, she felt confident enough to speak to a woman at her side.

"What's become of our host today?"

The woman spared a glance from the set of three-layered dominoes they were both watching. "He wanders about," she said. "Best to let him alone, I've found, until he's ready to talk to you."

A yelp came from behind them and a big, heavy man surged to his feet.

"That wasn't a cheat." He clutched his head with both hands. "I was just thinking sideways. I would never . . ."

A waiter came swiftly to his side. "Quite understandable, sir. The pain will ease off in an hour or two. If you'll just come with me."

He put an arm round the man and urged him from the room, through a nervous silence. Everyone else turned their gaze away and Cass forced herself to do the same.

Lunch was a buffet, set out in the dining room for guests to help themselves. Cass admired the architectural sketches, which had replaced the Victorian hunting scenes on the walls. She was impressed by the salads on their silver dishes, the eggs and smoked salmon set out in star patterns, the beef olives and fancy breads. Her mouth and stomach were too clenched for her to eat, however. She picked up a plate here, put it down there and took a glass of champagne, which she did not drink. She tagged onto a group, who finished their meal early and headed out of the room.

They led her into the Snakes and Ladders Room, where they settled down to games even more intense than elsewhere. "Join us," someone said and she played a round of Monopoly, with a London board and extra cards to send you into exile or on visits to the palace. Cass was the winner, which earned her an invitation to take on four of the losers at poker.

"How about we play this straight and forget old Moore's curlicues?" one asked. That suggested they were not bound by the spell, but maybe it was a trap. Cass kept her face blank, while the dealer, a lackadaisical man with a horseshoe tiepin, paused in his shuffling.

"You can do that anywhere, Bob. I come here for the curlicues." He raised an eyebrow at Bob, who shrugged.

"Up to you, Stringy."

The values of the court cards were reversed and new ones added, from a tarot pack. Three games later, Cass had a stack of chips, which she lost all on one hand to Stringy. He smiled at her.

"You're a quick thinker, young man. How about we play for a forfeit, just you and me, at any card game you like?"

Drumlin was in the room. Cass had spotted him on the deal before last and had been aware of his every movement since. He stood opposite her now, a little apart from the other onlookers.

"A fine proposition." She smiled at Stringy and spoke in her natural voice. "But I've already won my game." She stood up and pulled off her wig.

"Cassiopeia!" Drumlin's whisper turned heads all across the room. He straightened his arms and drew himself up to his tallest. "How did you get in?"

"I cheated, just as you expected," Cass said.

"Someone must have helped you."

"Must they?" The room was as quiet as a theatre at the height of a show. The guests stared as much at her as at Drumlin, their breath held, their games neglected in front of them.

"Tell me who brought you here." Drumlin's voice belonged

more in a courtroom than a theatre, slow and dark.

"Not I." Cass had no wish to make trouble for the kitchen staff. Let Drumlin worry about which of his guests he should blame. "I don't let down my friends."

"Then I'll find out later." The mood in the room changed from fascination to anxiety but Drumlin paid no attention. "You had better leave at once."

She could gaze her fill at him now, for the first time in five years. He was a touch thinner and tidier, his hair shorter, his jacket narrower. His eye sockets were deeper and the bones of his face closer to his skin. He was as good looking as ever but more austere than she remembered.

"You'll have to throw me out," Cass said, cheerfully. "It won't be a pretty sight for all this delightful company. And then you'll have to face the pictures I give to the papers tomorrow."

"You're not welcome in my home," Drumlin said. "Isn't that enough to make you go?"

None of her plans had taken her beyond this point. She was not up for a physical fight and to be dragged out of the house would be humiliating, however much she might relish the social consequences for Drumlin. But just to walk out at his bidding was too tame an end for her escapade.

"I'll make you an offer," she said. "Play one game against me, your choice. If you win, I'll leave quietly and never darken your doors again."

His stillness condensed into the tension of a hunting cat. "And if I lose?"

Cass looked around for inspiration. The company were stuck in discomfort by now, bulgy-eyed and open-mouthed. This room would make a fine space for dances on summer evenings, with a view through the long windows into the twilight garden. She had hankered after her lost chance to rearrange the castle, ever since she had walked out on Drumlin. "If you lose," she said, "the castle will be my home and you'll leave, until the day you can sneak back in without being caught."

If Drumlin had looked this bleak when they first met, Cass might never have dared to speak to him. "A game of chess," he said. "If you will play by my rules and be bound by my spell this once."

She was frightened of the spell. But if she refused, she would lose before they started. She nodded and kept her mind blank, while the necessary paraphernalia was fetched. She did not flinch when Drumlin marked her forehead, her mouth and her hands with invisible patterns. She spoke the words he told her, he muttered an incantation and she felt the spell take hold, like a net round her thoughts, gentle unless it was tightened.

The chess set was less showy than the one she had seen before but elegant, with Lalique pieces of clear and clouded glass.

"The usual moves," Drumlin said. "But whenever you lose one, you must give me a truthful answer to one question or forfeit the game."

"And vice versa?"

He pulled his head back, as though the alternative were unthinkable. "Of course."

They sat at a table in the middle of the room, with the crowd thick around them. Through a haze of cigarette smoke, Cass saw people craning in at the door. The windows were open but the air was too warm even so, filled with the scents of tobacco and expensive perfumes. Cass wished for her favourite sleeveless dress but at least she could take off her jacket and tie, which helped a little. She shook her head at a glass of champagne but accepted one of iced tea.

"What was your favourite toy, when you were six years old."

The obvious answer was the rag doll, which Cass had carried about. She opened her mouth to say so and felt the spell bristle. She thought harder. For years, her heart had belonged to a wooden carving she was seldom allowed to touch. Not a toy and not hers, except in her imagination. Maybe that was what counted for the spell. "My father's Chinese dragon," she said and the spell net subsided.

She refocused her thoughts and took one of Drumlin's pawns. "Who was your best friend when you were eleven?"

He scowled but answered with barely a pause. "My great aunt Jane."

Cass lost track of the time. The spectators were quiet and impartial, as far as she could sense, or at least too gripped by the tension to show their preferences. Drumlin's questions grew more subtly intrusive every time she lost a piece and she tried to match them, when she had the chance. Then he captured her rook.

"How did you get in today?"

She should have seen that coming. "As a plumber," she said. He sat back, staring in surprise. She smiled at him. "You'll find my bag downstairs."

That felt like a small triumph. But the chess game was going in

Drumlin's favour. Five moves later, he captured her knight.

"How many men have you slept with, since you left me?"

Someone in the audience gasped. "None," Cass said, furious that she dared not lie.

Exhaustion weighed her down and impatience with her failing strength. He could sense that she was in trouble, judging from the new gleam in his eyes and the shadow of a smile on his mouth. She had seen that look before. And suddenly, she knew how to stop him.

On her next move, she took one of his pawns. That put her queen in danger, but she did not care.

"Which woman here do you most want to sleep with tonight?" she asked.

He sat like a statue and she saw that she had been right. He wanted her, even after all these years, even sweaty and dishevelled from her disguise. He wanted her and he would not tell her so. "Your game," he said. The spell net dropped from her mind, as the sweep of his hand knocked the pieces off the board. "Your castle, until I find my way back in."

GELENA AND GOLD

Anthony C. Ermi

The door would not open. Maiman knocked, banged, kicked, and peered through the mottled glass, but nobody came to see him in. And yet he knew that the house *was* occupied: not by men or women or children, not dogs or cats or bats or rats. But occupied, "As sure as the sea shines," as they say in Dreamtide.

The chimney exhaled a thin stripe of woodsmoke into the breaking clouds, and the firelight deep inside the innermost hearth cast its golden glow upon the windows, upon Maiman himself. Soft music sung in a hundred little voices came from still deeper within; a merry sound that made him, despite all the anxiety now racking inside, wish for a nice pint of beer and jovial company to end out the day. It had been a long one, and as such days habit to do, it grew even longer as he stood there. Now he saw the persons inside, and none of them seemed the least bit like the one he sought. Of course, they had seen him too, heard all the knocks. One of the little lads grabbed onto the interior edge of the glass and poked its face, snaggletooth and all, right in front of Maiman's.

Maiman started back, grabbed for the sword on his waist, but did not yet unsheathe it; if an armed man cannot exercise patience, he should not be permitted arms at all. The door handle wiggled several times, as if some petite figure were grasping up at it and failing to gain a grip, before it swung open with a squeak. For a moment, nothing happened, and Maiman peered into the dim hallway, taking another step or two back. Then they all poured out onto the lawn. Dozens of little squatters, plump and stout and altogether strange. He had never met one for himself—a Yesterling—now he was practically swimming in the pudgy buggers.

They bounced all over each other as they dumped from the cottage and slid through the mud just outside, passing around Maiman's ankles and between his legs like salmon at laying season in an overflowing stream. He let his hand fall from his sword as he realized the only threat these creatures might pose would be to a beer keg, and he dodged the flood the best he could. Which was not very well. At first he tried apologizing to those who hit their heads the hardest against his greaves, but the human mouth and tongue are only capable of making so many sounds each second, and not nearly enough to accommodate the myriad of green bodies flailing about for grip, babbling exclamations in their home tongue, and passing out senseless from the excitement of it all.

The cottage was only capable of holding so many figures, no matter how small they were, so the flood soon slowed to a trickle. The last of the creatures to exit no longer slid because they were stumbling and falling, but slid because it seemed like, as they often said, *the jolly right thing to do.* One of these final Yesterlings had his jolly right slide interrupted by levitation and a feeling of freefall: Maiman grabbed him by the fluted collar of his shirt and held him up, face to face.

By some coincidence, the face of the lad Maiman grabbed was the same face he had been face to face with while his face and the little face were peering through the window. A real wallop of a sentence, he realized, even as he thought it out, but then again, Yesterlings are known to rub off their dialectic habits on those around them. This tends to wear off after a day or two. Some learned man in some big city came up with some fancy name for this phenomenon, but fancy things never much interested Maiman. He chalked it up to the Yesterlings being funny little fellows.

"Hello, funny little fellow," he said to the helpless Yesterling as it reached its stubby arms toward Maiman's gigantic hand without avail.

The thing roared, or squeaked, at first, then made a few sounds that might have been insults of terrific vehemence; it extended its snaggletooth to its full length much as a snake does its fangs—though this was one tooth at the very center of its upper jaw and was about as sharp as a thoroughly used pencil. When it receded, Maiman thought with a smile, the fellow would much resemble a child who just got his first baby-tooth knocked out on the playground. Though it is a fact that, despite its size, the Yesterling, to have a fully developed front tooth at all, must be over five-hundred years old . . . hence the name. Where had he learned that again? Oh, whatever.

Finally, the little fellow, still making all sorts of sounds, waned in his provocative tone and mellowed enough to drop into the standard tongue. This happened in the middle of a sentence, the vilest bits of which were cut off.

"...and I swear on the grave of Tessessa...that...that... you will regret handling me in this manner, this manner is far too mean for me, I can see!"

Apparently, the fellow was a man of some stature in the Yesterling hierarchy; but his subordinates, if subordinates they were, did not seem very interested in helping him escape the prison that was Maiman's gauntleted hand. He looked back over his shoulder and saw the most of them still rolling around in mud or ambling off down the hill and into the woods, probably to forage for Hopshrooms or to perform some other jolly right pastime, one of those listed out in Chief Metran's *Thirty-Six Jolly Right Pastimes*, published circa 7024. That was before the thirteen tribes of Yesteryear united, before the first coronation, before Selemen's doomed rebellion, before even the first delve into Lake Bygone!

What? Maiman shook his head. He did not know what any of that meant, nor why images of great feasts populated by drunk and drunkening Yesterlings pervaded his mind...nor even why he really, really wished to go and meander along a woodland stream at that very moment *(Jolly Right Pastime #23)*.

Maiman turned back to the little chap in his hand now, and saw a smirk along its flat face, a smirk that brought the dull snaggletooth almost to the bottom of its chin, a chin where a few stray white hairs hung on fear dear life. The little chap would be hanging on much the same if he didn't wipe that smile away, he thought. Maiman got the urge to shake the guy around a little, and he did so with a smile twice as broad.

"Alright! Alright! Stop it! Goodness, you just about sent my head rolling all the way back to Mount First, the Mountain that came first from the first stones, alright!" exclaimed the little grassy-green man, eyes looking all directions while at nothing in particular as he stopped shaking.

Maiman resisted an urge to see if he could punt the creature back to Mount Whatever, and said, "Why are you and your merry band inside this house?"

"Why are we here? Because the house has four walls, a fireplace, it has a fireplace, and it has four walls! It has a keg of beer in the pantry, and it has enough glasses for us to pass the glasses around and drink until we're on our asses!"

"You're all already on your asses." Maiman pushed a passed out and mud-coated Yesterling with his heel. "Where is the girl who lives here?"

"Girl? You mean the gold girl, the old girl; the throne girl, the stone girl? She is gone, long gone I fear, though we all did find that quite queer. No, she left when we came over the hills, and over the hills we all came. Gone now."

"Do you remember where this girl went?"

"She went over the hills and through the heather to places never touched by fern nor feather. Not here."

Weren't you supposed to kill a hostage when it ran out of usefulness? Maiman thought about that, and he also thought about rhymes and things that didn't quite rhyme. He hated rhymes.

"Okay," he said, slowly, careful not to let any jolly right rhymes slip into his speech. "How about I take your keg of beer, remove the stopper, and dump the whole thing on your head? Would that jog your memory? How about a few more shakes? I'll make you quake, you little snake!" *Damnit. Oh well.*

"No, no! Okay, she went out tither! The girl whose hair was of pearls, around whom the air liked to twirl, she and the others rode the wind that whirls to the place where things unfurled."

"Stop all the damned rhyme and talk to me as if I were swine! *Where* is this girl at this time?" He couldn't help himself.

"I would reckon she's in Myrl, this girl."

"Myrl."

"Yes. If you let me down, let me run along the ground like the free and lovely squirrel, I will take you there, to Myrl, take you to the girl."

Maiman thought about this for a moment, about the logistics of kicking several hundred bumbling fellows in their behinds, and settled for letting them act as guides. Rhymes, rhymes, rhymes— it was just one of those things that happened among the Yesterlings. Jolly right fellows, they were, though it took Maiman some time to come to that conclusion.

By the third day of travel, the third day in which they reached no place called Myrl, Maiman realized that the Yesterlings were leading him on the proverbial 'wild goose chase'. He had told them about how urgent his business was, how he needed to speak with the girl, Galena, about matters pertaining to life and death, but Chulii, the leader of this gaggle of Yesterlings, responded in some cryptic rhyme about the sky and flies and goodbyes, and only ran along ahead, the little staff he carried held high like that of a shepherd. In a way, he was a shepherd.

Travel, for these creatures, was more akin to a landslide than any human mode of transport. Through the forests, over tangled roots, down gentle slopes and up the sides of perilous cliffs, the collective surged almost as one, bodies groping and tumbling and leaping and bounding. Maiman could see no ground beneath the mob. He tried to count them once as they walked, and came up with the number ninety-two. It seemed right. When he re-counted an hour later, he got the number one hundred and five.

The Yesterlings liked to set camp at twelve-hour intervals: once at midday when they napped and drank and talked, and much the same at midnight, where they slept a little more, drank a little more, and talked a little more. There was always talk. They talked in their sleep. They talked while others were sleeping. They talked while Maiman was relieving himself— they talked *about* Maiman relieving himself.

But it was hard to be mad at them. Their tongues were loose and their secrets looser. By second camp on the first day of travel, he knew all about how their home had been ransacked by crea-tures they called Red-Deer; how Chulii and his group had been in one of the deeper delves of their community's cave—every community of Yesterlings, of course, had a cave, wherein they planted and sowed their Hopshrooms, brewed their Hopshroom ales, drank their Hopshroom tankards, thought about how the next Hopshroom harvest would come out—and thus heard the carnage above and had time to escape. They had run single file (something Maiman thought a little hard to believe as he watched them travel now) through forgotten mineshafts that led into deeper bowels of Mount First, places even older than the Yesterlings, dug out by civilizations so ancient they no longer have names to be called. These sections ran all the way to the rear of the great mountain and spilled them out into the valley beyond. They had seen the Red-Deer leaving the scene with their spoils lit by moonlight, huge burlap sacks hanging from their shoulders: but they did not divulge any more than this. That did not mean, however, that Maiman didn't *know* more than this. He saw images sometimes, learned things that he should not have learned, just as had when he first met them. It was not all pleasant. He had the impression that the attack on Mount First was not finished, that the Red-Deer had not stolen all they wished to steal.

When they walked, Chulii led the way. Or at least seemed to lead the way. Others spilled in front of him sometimes much like children on their way home from school, heading just as sure toward their destination. That destination—not Myrl, of course— must have been Mount First. Maiman surmised that *Myrl* was a place entirely fictional, contrived just to rhyme with *girl*. Silly. Whenever Maiman asked how many days of travel Chulii antici- pated, the latter would say something along the lines of:

"A good adventure is as good as the goodest medicine, my good friend. Nothing but a good beer is gooder." Not quite a rhyme, but he reckoned that the Yesterlings were not grammatical scholars or poets. They loved their alliteration and repetition just as much.

Whenever Chulii finished speaking to Maiman, he would skip along ahead and take up a travel song, of which the Yesterlings seemed to have many for a historically sedentary people. They did not have many supplies, though. They went on without provisions, without stores of water, without sleeping bags or tents or thicker jackets in case of rain; they had no maps, no compasses, no tools with which to start a fire or lay a real camp. But they did have songs.

When they stopped, it was Maiman that lit the flames; it was Maiman who roasted the rabbits he'd caught on their walks; it was Maiman who shared his scanty provisions. The Yesterlings, though they ate with mirth anything he might provide, did not seem dejected when he told them he had not enough to spare, however— they contented themselves with just their waterskins. Waterskins he knew were filled with ale.

On the fourth day out, Maiman finished the last of his water. They had not passed a stream since they left the bank of the one by the cottage three days before. The land on which they walked was hard-packed and rocky, the roots of the myriad trees breaching through the thin but tough top layer of soil or scrambling over half-covered boulders here and there. By no means was Maiman the type to keel over and pass out after a day or two without water, but he had only brought with him the one waterskin and had been rationing it over the previous days. When noon came around and they set on the side of a hill under the unrelenting sun, he tried in vain to squeeze another drop or two from the waterskin before letting himself sleep, half-expecting to die of heat-stroke or dehydration in his armor before he awoke. When he did wake, it was with two new skins of pungent ale laying at his side, his own filled to the brim. He never knew which of the Yesterlings put them there, and he never asked.

When rains did come, the creatures threw their overcoats over his sleeping frame, even though his full set of silver-alloy armor provided more-than-ample protection. When a river came that they could not cross, it was the Yesterlings that pushed over the nearest tree and laid a bridge. When wolves passed by in the shadows of night, it was the Yesterlings who put up a racket and drove the beasts whimpering into the forest. The Yesterlings were not the usual type. They were not any type at all. They were the Yesterlings, and they did things by their own methods and for their own reasons. They shared all they had, did all they could— but only within the bounds of their knowledge. Maiman would say that they knew their strengths, their weaknesses, their place in the world, but he was not so sure about that. It seemed almost as if they *didn't* know: anything at all.

What was war to a Yesterling? What was the balance of power between the three nations of Eastwing Bay? What was the rise of Celenano and his subsequent assassination, the degeneration of relations between Dreamtide and Mothersun? They were supposed to be a mythical people, these Yesterlings, but they did not seem to know that. They did not seem to care, or even recognize, that their near-endless lifespans were an aberration among living things. They did not know that humans had been trying for centuries to recreate their ale-brewing techniques to no avail. No. The Yesterlings knew drink, they knew joy, they knew song, they knew dance, and they knew companionship. Nothing more, at least that Maiman could see. The first day had been a frustrating one indeed, but since then, they treated him as one of their own. They did not give him side-eye glances or ask him questions about a culture that must have been extremely varied from their own— they plodded along the trail, told him to watch his step over ledges and tangles, and marched around him as if he was just a few feet tall himself.

It took Maiman a while to realize, but he did not care anymore that they told him nothing about where they were going—clearly, Chulii had some plan in mind for him, even if he would not tell it. A man who served none but his liege and his betrothed, a man who had fought and bled for his flag more times than he could count, trudging along as equals with a band of whosits and whatsits from the nation of wheresits on a mission to do . . . well, he was still wondering about the whysits and the howsits of it all. Maybe the Yesterlings wanted him to help reclaim their homeland. Maybe salvage their stolen items. Maybe enact revenge against those who wronged them. He didn't quite know, but he would see. He would help them.

Maiman's speech no longer fell into the rhyming dialect of the Yesterlings, but the other 'symptoms' he had developed throughout his time with the strange leaf-colored people only continued to intensify. At one point after noon on the sixth day, one of the Yesterlings fell and hit his head. Now, this had not seemed a very abnormal incident to Maiman when he saw it; the Yesterlings' preferred method of movement involved the repeated bashing of their heads against the ground as an unavoidable side-effect. But the fellow, Fubpi, did not have his tooth extended at the moment of impact. It turns out, as Maiman learned (though he did not *learn* it, necessarily, more so acquired the knowledge out of the air), that this tooth was not a tooth at all. Instead, it was some sort of pressure valve for the brain, admitting it less space to bobble around inside the thick and short skulls of the Yesterlings by changing the air dynamic of the little space inside. Or something like that.

Fubpi had leaped off the back of another Yesterling and hit a tree branch above, right on the forehead. If that wasn't enough, the back of his head landed flat on a stone, and Maiman saw the blood, as green and resplendent as melted-down emeralds, before anything else. All at once the group stopped, even those at the very front who could not have possibly witnessed the event— and a terrible sense of loss came over everyone. Came over Maiman. He felt the fear of Chulii, the guilt of the Yesterling who Fubpi leaped from, the shock of all those around. It passed like something palpable, like a vapor on the air, something that all breathed in at once and all felt in perfect synergy. Other things leaked too, in this moment of shared weakness: Maiman knew things then, happenings in personal history, memories of memories of memories. It was almost indescribable— it was as if he was a fly and looked at each of the hundred Yesterlings' minds through a segment of his multifaceted eyes, and all were presented at once and in full. Their youths, oh-so-long ago; their occupations; their trifles; their sufferings; their loves.

Fubpi recovered quick. What happened to him might have been classified as a major concussion if he were to be taken to a human doctor, but Yesterlings tended to base things on what they saw. They saw bruises on both sides of his head, yes, but Fubpi stood up only minutes after, and was walking soon after that. The first thing he said when he awoke was, "Sorry to worry you all! All you all must have been scared, you all! Things are jolly right!"

And they were off again, stumbling and bumbling and tumbling. Maiman laughed.

On the night of the seventh day of travel, something in the disposition of the Yesterlings changed, and Maiman felt that as well—a stone fortress around their hearts, around *his* heart. But he observed it too. The Yesterlings' songs were not quite as loud, as if they feared someone listened from beyond the oaks. Their drink was reserved, only a few small sips each to stave away anxieties. They did not skip, they did not hop, they did not dance, they did not bound over one another. They plodded along almost somberly, almost despondently, shying away from the shadows as they deepened.

Maiman went to Chulii after he set the fire. The leader was sitting on a stump, tossing a small stone between his even smaller hands.

"Oh, human. Hello," Chulii said.

"Hello, Chulii. Is there something wrong tonight?" Of course, he already suspected their proximity to the mountain, already saw strange and fleeting images in his mind of sprawling catacombic passages, of terrible eyes staring down from causeways layered high near the summits above. The figures behind these eyes, lanky and imposing, repeated a lonesome word over and over, but he could not quite make out what it was.

"We will arrive on the morrow. Hearts, tonight, are heavy with worry. There is a group-thought among us that we cannot shake."

"And what is that, my friend?"

The little man frowned. If not for the wispy white hairs on his chin and head, he would have looked awfully like a disappointed toddler, his balled and pudgy fist now set beneath his jaw.

"When we . . . left." It was the first time any of the little men had discussed this event with him directly. There were no rhymes. "When we left, we did so under unfavorable conditions. There is a doubt in all our minds to if our fellows, our brothers and sisters, if they still live. We cannot . . . well, I know not if you would understand, but we cannot *feel* them. They are not there, in our heads."

It is true: he didn't understand. But he had learned by now, and had felt himself, the group-think on display within the party. They were not a hivemind. They were individuals with personalities, with egos, with desires (though mostly for drink and mirth)— yet their thoughts, their feelings, their memories, all seeped, seeped through the air. He felt it then, more than ever before: the collective dread among the beings. It hurt. A wilted flower, a butterfly with clipped wings. They should not despair, such happy people.

"It does not," Chulii went on, "necessarily mean that they are . . . gone. Just that they are not projecting. They are obscured, perhaps looking in a different direction. Let's see . . ." The Yesterling searched for some metaphor that Maiman would understand. "A window at the front of a house cannot see the children playing in the backyard. It is so?"

"It is."

"Jolly right. Yes, it is the same with us. Perhaps we are in the backyard and they are at the window, or the other way around. Perhaps we are both in opposite yards or both at separate windows. Perhaps we are in separate houses altogether. We could be looking in the same place, projecting the same things, and both of our calls would fall on no ears. This is how it is, and that is why we weep today. As tomorrow, we will know for sure."

But the door to the house was left open. All that night as they slept under the silver-white starlight, it was with a cool draft of air seeping from outside, almost unbeknownst. Tomorrow would come sooner than they hoped.

Maiman awoke some time past the darkest hour of night, sat

upright and squinted into the darkness. It seemed that the stars had gone out, that all in the world held its breath or had shied away in silent terror. But the Yesterlings stirred. Maiman felt it, though he did not yet hear or see them. His vision flashed and images came across of a shared terror. A shared terror that had come again.

He heard the things coming before he saw them— in what felt like an instant, the forest became a cacophony of thumping, clopping, stomping hooves. He shot up from the camp, grabbed his scabbard, and ran to the near edge of the clearing, wherefrom, hazy in the distance, came the light of bobbing, flickering, sapphire-blue torches.

Over the past several days of travel Maiman had ruminated much on the idea of these Red-Deer, the nondescript, faceless adversary that the Yesterlings had been all but destroyed by. Perhaps it was a mispronunciation of the word 'raider,' or maybe a physical description of their appearance—he knew now that the truth was somewhere in the middle. Maybe he would have realized earlier if his mind had been wholly his own . . . but in any case, realization came now.

He could not see the hairy legs, the hooved feet, the paper-thin bodies, the all-too long arms, the pointed faces, the terrible claws; but he could see the antlers like a procession of fractal skeletons marching to an unheard melody, lit only by the pale-blue licks of flame atop every pinnacle of contorted bone. Intravenous spermaceti pumped as through winding rivers, spilled at deltas of cold heat and colder light, stole the safety of night's darkness and did not give it back. These same fires heralded the end of the last age. The same chaunt that brought down dynasties now echoed in the trees, silenced any Yesterlings still chittering.

The nightmare creatures crept over fallen leaves with steps lighter than air, louder than thunder. They held their staves upon mighty shoulders, stamped them on the ground to dispel any ancient wards that might block their path. They sang, but it was not the joyous melody of the Yesterlings: they sang a monotonous and tuneless phrase, over, over, over again.

Reitere, Reitere, Reitere, the things said in quivering, clicking, sputtering vocalizations. *Reitere, Reitere, Reitere.*

Nobody had translated it a thousand years ago when the creatures stormed the capitals of all six allied kingdoms, and nobody translated it for the next five-hundred years in which the creatures were a rare, but *very real,* threat, not until they receded back into the earth from whence they came. Words are only words. Only when the creatures became subjects of legendry did people even attempt translation, did they search back in annals of forgotten kingdoms, in runes scrawled on the oldest megalithic stones, in the pages of locked-away esoterica to find the root tongue, the unholy syllables they spoke. Who knew one word could hold so much meaning? Maiman wished he didn't know. But now all the images that had flashed upon him from the little men clarified, brightened, gained definition.

The *Red-Deer.* The reitere. They trailed before him, a dozen or more, images plucked straight from a thousand years of the world's collective nightmares. They seemed unarmed but for their huge triple-bladed claws, but he knew that meant little; these were the only weapons they ever needed to slay the greatest armies ever assembled by mankind. Besides, fear was weapon enough, and the Yesterlings did not seem like choice warriors even at the best of times. This was not the best of times.

Limbs waved low to the ground like broken tree branches, eyes blazed where moonlight could never reach, wafts of death stench came over the bracken. Maiman made a motion for the rest to remain silent, but the threshold of noise so many people in one spot could make was not low enough. Someone moved, or gasped, or sobbed—Maiman didn't even hear. But the reitere did. One turned its head, not even a hundred feet away. Blue eyes stared like sapphire flames. Another set joined. And another. Chills ran over Maiman as he locked stares with the horde of devils, and he grasped the handle of his sword slowly. The chaunt went silent, as did all else . . . all else except the flicker of those terrible flames. His mind refused to work. But his body cooperated just fine. It took him several moments to realize why he was doing it, but he pulled off his helmet, his breastplate, his leggings, and began to dig into the loose soil with his hands. He stuffed the silver armor into the hole, threw the dirt back atop it, and finally dared to look up. The eyes were gone. The noise was not.

Reitere, Reitere, Reitere.

Sibilant, it hung on the air as the reitere traveled from never to forever. Maiman did not leave the forest edge that night.

Before dawn, Maiman dozed—a sleep laced with vague scenes of snoring Yesterlings and thoughts of how thankful he was that the night had not taken a different turn. If he had unsheathed his sword, if he hadn't remembered to remove and hide his armor . . . well, maybe the night would have.

The Ishmans believe that the reitere were sent by gods of the ground to reclaim the resources stripped by humanity, and their actions certainly aligned with this idea. Even now, even in times when the creatures had become merely a remembered name, most travelers left their golden watches and silver pendants locked in their chests when they needed pass through the wilderness. Maybe not so much in the cities, but out in the sticks where the legend of the night thieves, the reclaimers, the reitere, persisted, the practice had not faded.

In brief interludes of sleep between panicked check-ups on his small friends and the near foliage, Maiman saw images of castle walls deconstructed, thrones melted by undying flames, coronas stripped of all their gems, great gilded towers toppled and left to rot. The reclaimers kept some of their spoils, brought them back into the earth from which they crawled chaunting and flaming, but left much more burned and desolate. They had passed him by, all the little impoverished and unarmed Yesterlings by, simply because he had not drawn his sword, because he had been quick enough to strip his defenses. There was a message there that he only just understood between the haze of sleep.

When Maiman awoke the sun was a little higher than he would have liked in the sky, and the pommel of his sword had left a big red indent on his cheek where he had leaned on it. The little men had gathered most of the bivouac (their personal effects, which consisted of their waterskin, a basket or two, a shawl, and various gathering tools suited to one's proficiency or preference) and were huddled together at the center of the clearing. Chulii spoke therein.

"…and the Red-Deer, they did, they did, they steered away and went. Where from? Where to? Who says. But not here, those

Deer. Elsewhere, to give others fear. That is my fear. Are these they who killed our friends? Are these they that came upon us? Who says. Who can say. Not me, nay. But I say— they shall kill others, perhaps today!"

A babble of affirmations and claps went up as the Yesterlings spun around each other like coffee grounds in a stirred mug. They held up spades and paring knives and hatchets with blades the size of Maiman's fingers, waved them in the air.

"We must follow the Red-Deer! We are not fighters, it is true, but when backs are to the wall, when it is fight or be killed, that is when the meager must put aside their fears and their predispositions!" Chulii shouted in fairly sophisticated prose. He was trembling.

"When we dig, we dig because the stone is in our way. When we build, it is because we must put something in the way of something else. When we run, we run because something is trying to put something in us. Chulii says, and Chulii is I, that we will fight before we let more die!"

Maiman rose then, walked through the crowd of Yesterlings, and into the center of the circle. All eyes drifted to him and lost some of their fire. He leaned down, wrapped his hand around Chulii's little raised first, and slowly lowered it. Tears came from the little eyes on the little man's face.

The group went on. By sundown they saw Mount First on the horizon. There were no lights.

Maiman dreamed a memory.

"Maiman," someone whispered.

He rose from sleep—within the dream itself—with a jolt and looked around disoriented for a moment, before he realized that whoever was speaking to him was doing so from outside the barracks.

There was a tap at the open window. "Maiman."

"Galena?" he asked as he rubbed the sleep from his eyes. "What . . . what are you doing here?"

"Come this way— there is something I must show you." A silver smile appeared on her golden face, and Maiman suddenly felt very naked in his bed without his armor.

"Princess, it is far too late for anything like this. Please, go back to bed—"

Next thing he knew he had been pulled out the window. Galena dragged him by the wrist through the interweaving gardens of Fort Dreamtide, and he thought all the while about how closely the she resembled the roses and tulips they passed as the moonlight hit her scarlet hair. Or was it golden? He could not tell. He did not want to.

The princess must have precontrived their way, as they missed every guard post, slipped beneath every window, and were soon running together down the large lawn outside the southwestern gate, Galena still grasping his arm. He ran now in perfect stride with her, but he did not ask her to remove her hand.

Sparse cottages and farms dotted the rolling and largely empty hills just outside the fort, and they ran in the valleys between these hills; valleys sufficiently illumined by the sunlike moon, valleys where deer scattered as the couple came, ran with antlers gleaming back to the woods they called home. There were no stars this night, such was the glow of the nearby sea of Dreamtide, but Maiman felt the starlight there as he watched *his* sun burn through the dark, burn so bright that it hurt his eyes to stare. Yet he could do nothing but.

They passed through fields of lightning lilies and plots of budding wheat, crossed over streams that he imagined served as thresholds to lands of fairy majesty to which he and the princess could run away; and his wish was not entirely lost.

After some thirty minutes, they came to a slope that fell steeper, followed by a river that whispered softer, than all the rest. Skipping from stone to stone, gasping yet smiling, they descended to a place covered by yawning willow trees. A small pool lay rippling at the bottom of the stream that fed it, and the slow gurgle of water on water accompanied Galena as she let go of Maiman's arm and knelt there.

Galena began to speak. She whispered low, under the underneath of her breath. The air began to tremble, motes of light began to dance and die around her. The ripples in the water changed their direction, began to come from the very center as if a stone had just fallen in, and the princess' hair, usually fiery enough, began to actively glow and cast a crimson, or maybe golden, light upon the scene.

Then she stood up just as abruptly as she had knelt, and turned to look at Maiman. The sun was in her eyes.

"Our lives are small, Maiman. We live in a brief fragment of a brief moment, loathing that another must come. Nothing visible, not youth, not possessions, not beauty, can last forever— but there are things, my love, that cannot be taken away. Not by anyone. And it is in these things that we must place our faith when all else fails. Across the mountains, through the deserts, in the deepest pits, none can strip the worth that we propagate."

Shimmering in the pool of water, Maiman saw a small cottage on a small hill, brown on green and green on brown. Princess Galena turned and walked atop the pond, treading its surface as sure as she might a path. Surer, even. She stood now just over the door.

"It is undeniable now, that the kingdom is in crisis. Times will soon come when the things we take for granted will be lost. I see this on the horizon, just cresting and bobbing far off on the lucent sea, but these times *will* come, and we must be ready when they do. And so, we must learn. We must, all of us, remember what we have forgotten. What mercantilism, militarism, fanaticism, and all our other follies have stripped away. Man was not meant to live in stone and fight with steel, and I will go to where no such things exist.

"Follow me, my love, follow me beyond the thumb we have placed upon ourselves. Dark skies may wait between then and now, and many moons might wax and wane, but we shall meet again in the place where value is valueless. Until that time, until we meet beneath the world or above, breathe in the light. Until that time, see with new sight. Until that time, guard what is pure when you deem it right."

Onto the mirage of the cottage stepped Princess Galena of Dreamtide. When she disappeared in a flash of dazzling light, so did half of Maiman's heart. And yet, as he walked back to the fort in a daze, staring up at the moon, all he thought about was light, sight, bright. To wax into rhyme at such an important moment . . . Maiman laughed, but he did not then understand.

All day Maiman found himself lost in thought, drifting on the dream-tide of memories and letting the emotions he had stifled come back over him: by the looks of things, and by the vague impressions his mind picked up, the Yesterlings did much the same.

Progress had been slow this day, and they did not make it all the way to the mountain. When the gloaming came, they set camp just at the foot of Mount First, but the thread of the night unwound through more somber silence, many of the Yesterlings sitting and watching the moon as it illuminated the crags and overhangs where they once roamed. Maiman saw the outlines of cutouts in the stone that might have been houses, might have been entrances into delves, and might have been nothing at all. But the little men knew. They knew who carved the cutouts, if cutouts they were; they knew who carried the stones from the deep mines; they knew who, with pick and chisel, dug the stones from the earth. The shadow of memory literally hung over them against the moonlight, a stark black triangle of doubt. They lit no fires.

When they began to walk in the morning, Chulii did so at Maiman's side. "Did you know, human, that Mount First is the first mountain, and that Mount First was first? Nowhere else on the continent is there a mountain that came firster."

The sun was pale and white above, and it shined down on an old path of cobblestone that they came across soon after setting out.

"It looks the part," Maiman said as they climbed, looking up at the shelves of rock.

"It does, and things are often as they do. Before there were tribes, before there was man, before there was us, before there was anything smarter than the wolves that pass in night, this mountain rose up. It rose, it danced, it spewed flame, it cooled, and it tapered. Taper, baper, snaper . . . why do you think mountains rise?"

Maiman thought about it, and watched the little man trot along, raising his staff to bark silent orders that went unheeded by the mob behind them. Despite their mind's best efforts, sight of their home in glorious daylight brought back the Yesterlings' good humor.

"Well," began Maiman. "The priests say—"

"No, no. That is not what you think. That is what others thought *for* you. Before, they thought, and now you speak without thinking, much like the parrot. You are chirp chirp chirping, not think think thinking."

He did not know what a parrot was, but Chulii's brain passed a colorful smudge of a bird over the void between them.

"Thinking," said Chulii, taking a swig of his ale. "Thinking is much like winking, or even drinking. I drink because I see the waterskin, and I feel the dryness of my mouth. I feel the sun upon my skin, and I do not like the heat. My body tells me it needs water— and yet I drink ale. But I see the ale, that it is like water, and I feel what it does to my tongue and my body, and I know that it is much the same. That it is better. I think that. I thought it. I do it. We drink, and wink, and blink. Thinking."

The cobblestones had long since faded back into overgrowth, but Chulii climbed on invisible pathways that he knew by habit, by instinct. The others followed just as quick, handspringing up ledges they could not reach or forming living bridges by connecting their legs and arms. Maiman was a little slower. His armor weighed him down, and he was no stellar climber to begin with. But as he watched the jubilant homecoming— he thought.

He thought about Galena. About his quest, if you will, the three-month journey across wastelands and wildernesses beyond description. The last week had carried with it a sense of the fantastic so pungent that he had almost, in some part of himself, forgotten— but duty never left. Galena never left. Not for a moment. When she had gone, he whispered as much to the dark pond she left behind. Now he whispered it again, turned and looked back across the land over which he crossed.

It was noon. The forest behind stretched endless, reaching over distances incalculable and showing trees innumerable. He could not see the castles of home, nor the signs of any settlement, village, or even a lone cottage like the one at which he met the Yesterlings.

"Hey!" Someone shouted from above.

Maiman looked up to see all the Yesterlings at a small doorway in the stone, crouching around it, crouching atop one another, crouching almost above open air at times. All of them were waiting for him, smiles on their faces, feet dancing around with anticipation like children at a candy shop. He nodded to himself, loosened the straps on his armor and let it fall to the ground. Such an act would leave him headless back in Dreamtide. But he was not in Dreamtide.

It had not been an easy decision, and even as he began to climb to where the Yesterlings waited, he debated inside. But when he reached them, his little friends, and felt them all gather around his legs, he knew he picked correctly. He had called them *creatures* when he first met them. What a terrible word he had chosen. Each of them was just as much a man as he—perhaps more. No, he knew now what a *creature* truly was. Never would he make that mistake in categorization again.

The Yesterlings had thought of him as one of their own since they first set out, and showed that through countless acts of kindness. Maiman admitted to himself there, for the first time, as he moved his hands from one stone to the next, that he felt a duty toward these little men. That he felt, without any reservation, like one of them.

This entrance was without signage—a narrow and dark staircase that went straight down into rock. Maiman followed close behind the Yesterlings as they piled downward, and he contented himself by listening to the sounds of their joy. A song went up, and its words were of family, new and old. Their sorrow had been short-lived indeed, and it left no traces when it went.

But it did leave seeds. And those seeds just needed the tiniest drop of liquid fear to sprout fruit. Maiman kicked himself for letting the little men grow so raucous in a place that might yet be hostile—when at last they emerged into a level space, a dark and expansive chamber, it came upon them without any of the hesitation the others had shown. A reitere.

Why it had remained, Maiman wondered long afterward. Perhaps it was left to guard the spoils until its fellows returned to finish the job. Why it attacked when they had no metals or riches exposed, he could not fathom. Perhaps it just wanted to kill. And though he felt it then, he could not quite assign words to the answers for several years. After many more adventures and many more daunting encounters, it came to him one day while he was drifting off the coast of Dreamtide, watching the resplendent waves split against the shore. Wealth is not always material.

The thing ignited its antlers as Maiman walked into the chamber; it jumped off a large column and its dastardly hook-claws gleamed in the light. Maiman didn't even have time to inhale before he had his sword out, gleaming just as bright, flashing through the air with those claws— sparks flew over the heads of the Yesterlings as the blades connected, and the little men went scrambling out into the darkness. Maiman could do no more than hope that there was only one.

Silver met black and made red. The claws of the creature were much like sickles; he had heard they used them to strip valuables from hard-to-reach places, or simply to destroy whatever they needed to destroy. It needed to destroy Maiman, and it flailed at him as might a huge and furious mantis.

Dreamtide was home to many of the greatest knights in the world, and Maiman had dueled and beaten many of them throughout his career. Never had he been pushed so close to his limit as this moment, against this strange, almost demonic creature. Its eyes blazed blue and the light flickered atop the branching antlers with every leap, every stride. From the left— he dodged back. Down below now— he parried. By the time he drew back his sword, the reitere had already adjusted and raised both arms to strike from above. It fought like hell.

But Maiman had seen hell. Maiman had been there and back, almost not metaphorically. The sickles clove a few spots through his clothes, the mouth full of crisscrossing teeth clove a few spots in his mind, but he struck the thing. It reared after one of Maiman's ripostes, leaped back upon its pillar, and launched itself through the air like a flaming, shrieking missile; Maiman sidestepped, swung at the neck, but missed— instead slicing off an antler and instantly igniting the fuel inside, making a flaming arc of his slash. The resin stuck to his sword there a moment, and it burned in the darkness. The reitere felt with its three fingered and far-too-long arm at the spot where Maiman cut it; flaming oil ejected in arterial spurts from the wound.

The reitere leaned back on its rear hoofed legs and almost collapsed, made a sound as of frying pans clapping together. In this moment Maiman stole a glance around the room, saw only a few quivering Yesterlings peering around corners and columns, others unconscious on the floor, and looked back just in time to see it: the true form of the creatures who had almost ended the reign of humanity, almost snuffed out the poor and helpless Yesterlings. From every pore, every orifice, every spot of flesh, it began to seep. Oil. Until the whole lanky creature was soaked, until a pool of the stuff spread across the flagstones and seeped into the cracks there. Maiman stood dumbfounded at first, but a flash or two of past horror blazed through his mind and he leaped backward. The creature folded back its lips, its entire jaw, and opened its mouth wide, too wide, like a python trying to fit a rat down its gullet, distending and disconnecting tissue as it went. And then— it snapped with the force of a hammer on an anvil. One spark was all it took. What once was a living creature, however terrible, in a burst of blue light, became an incarnate devil of fire. Its image was projected threefold onto the ground, walls, and columns; its height was now well over two meters; its horns, now with uncountable branches and endings, reached up into space that would have been entirely shadowed if not for the nauseating light they produced.

And then the fire pounced, and the fire snapped with teeth of radiating plasma, and the fire left a wake of sulphur fumes where it had been. When it swiped, a solar flare crashed across Maiman's chest. When it bounded, a trail of ignited air burned in its wake. When it reared up, all the Yesterlings shouted and cowered, shying from the harsh light.

There was a book popular among children in Maiman's hometown, one of those books that they hid under their beds and hoped that their parents never looked for. The *Elmo Bestiarium*. It was said to be a retranslated and abridged edition of a much longer work by one of the foundational wizards of Hyprisse before its destruction: the kids, him included, never cared much for the words, the esoterica therein, but— on page 132, Maiman still remembered, there was marked in dark blue ink, a crude drawing of what the author claimed was a *discordant cave spirit*. That image now stood over him. Maiman was on his knees, red welts and burns covering much of his face and body.

The creature came up slow, relishing its victory, its flaming antlers blazing in the dark; when it stood over Maiman, infernal breath wafting against his face like superheated sewer steam. He put his sword up, the only defense he had left. It was not enough. The creature—the *creature*—grabbed the blade with its bare, flaming hand, and melted it. The silver softened, became malleable, and in one swift movement, the reitere tossed a huge glob of the stuff, half the blade, over its shoulder. Then it pressed itself overtop him, the reitere, and lowered its sneering, massive mouth, to go for the kill.

Maiman turned his head and looked out into the darkness around him. There were a few bodies of fright-passed-out Yesterlings nearby, but he looked past them. He looked Chulii in the eyes, knowing just where he would be in the vastness of the room.

Maiman said, or rather thought, to the little, fern-colored, gap-toothed man who gave him drink when he thirsted, joy when the nights were cold, and friendship when he needed it most and expected it least: "I'm sorry."

Maiman may have only been unconscious for a handful of seconds, but that he regained consciousness at all surprised him enough— that the reitere was no longer upon him was an even greater surprise.

The creature's fire had gone out and it stood at its original height. And it was reeling. It roared at something in the shadows, dodged something that flew through the air, flung something that had climbed onto its back, and seemed, to Maiman's (albeit dazed) perspective, to be in a full retreat. It reached a back wall, roared a few more times as its assailants continued their push, before it lit the fires on its antlers as bright as Maiman had yet seen them— it lashed a few whips of flame around itself to give luft and snapped its neck back. It headbutted the solid stone floor. There came a burst of blue light and heat as the top layer of rock melted and turned to magma— and then the reitere was gone. Dived into the very mountain itself.

A cheer went up from the Yesterlings as they poured back into the center of the chamber, and the sound echoed all up in the high vaults of what certainly could not have been a structure dug by their people. It was a strange time for it, but Maiman felt a surge of memories then: but not memories of the Yesterlings. Memories the Yesterlings *inherited*. It struck him, the true power these men possessed— they could live a thousand years, meet millions of people— and from all of them, even those forgotten by short-lived mankind, they could keep some of their memories. Each Yesterling was a vault of priceless information, of history none considered reachable again. He had reached it. He saw those who had dug out this chamber: huge men, well over seven feet tall each, huge hammers, huge armors, huge weapons. And then the vision faded.

Chulii ran to Maiman's side and knelt, gently touched a burned spot on his shoulder. A strange and rusted helmet leaned on the top of the Yesterling chief's head. A huge helmet.

"Human! Are you living?" he asked.

Maiman nodded, or maybe grunted.

Chulii rose and did a little jig, circled around Maiman and whooped. "We defeated it, see! We did it! We defeated it, beated it, nearly turned it to meat, we did! Jolly right! Jolly right!"

"You . . . ?" Maiman looked around as if a great warrior might remain hidden among the ranks of Yesterlings . . . one of his fellow Dreamtide knights, perhaps. All he saw were short and chubby men with gaps between their teeth and rusted and pitted spears in their hands, rotted bows and pointless arrows, all far too large for their statures, all reappropriated from the armory of the Huge Men that had called Mount First home before their people ever arrived, ever expanded the tunnels they found. Behind the Yesterlings' tattered armor and helmets, behind their usual leather attire, they all wore bright and bubbly smiles.

Maiman rose with help from Chulii and a few others, and walked across the chamber under his own power. The wounds hurt like all hell, but they were nothing more than surface burns at most, nothing fatal or incapacitating. He looked around at the devastation, at the molten pit into which the reitere fled, and laughed.

"You," he said after a couple breaths, "I was not sure about you folk when we set out last week. I thought you raucous, unserious, incoherent, simple, and altogether unfit to be travel companions; and though I have confirmed that you are more than one of those things, you are also utterly unique. Dreamtide would benefit from a few more folk with your disposition, I tell you what. No amount of shining armor and razorblade swords can change the heart of a soldier, change the way his mind works. If the whole world were more like you, perhaps the ghosts of the past would pose no more threat to anyone. Thank you all for saving my life. Thank you, Chulii. I am sorry I could not better protect you."

The little men started dancing long before Maiman finished and they continued long after he did; but they did move on. They had few lights to ward off the darkness, but the smiles of the Yesterlings shined the way well enough. As they went, Chulii came to Maiman's side as he often did.

"You know, human," he said. "I did not bring you along to be our protector. Yesterlings have never wanted protectors or vectors or inspectors. You are nothing of the sort, my friend . . . you are . . . let's say . . . a projector!" And the little man danced away without any elaboration. Maiman knew not to ask for any. He did not need it.

Maiman waited for another creature to appear from the shadowed places above as they followed the hall that led out from the gigantic chamber, but soon those shadowed places disappeared altogether as the corridor grew narrower, lower, newer. The ceiling that before hung so far above his head, he could now reach out and touch. This section was the perfect height for the little Yesterlings.

The path curved this way and that and had a thousand little branches, but the Yesterlings chose the way on with decision, knew which branch went where and for how long to follow the branch before it branched off again into another branch branching. Maiman no longer hated the quirks that snuck into his thoughts at times. They did not meet another reitere.

Soon enough the bends and branches in the corridor faded away and it ran straight through the rock, tilting slightly up or down here and there. As they reached this straightaway, the Yesterlings lost the battle against patience and broke into top speed, disappearing into the thick darkness. Maiman tried his darnedest to keep up, smiling against his pain and against his usual nature, but most of the party outpaced him. What enigmatic little fellows. To think he had almost throttled their leader upon their first meeting . . . how quickly things change! He was reminded as he walked through the bowels of this tunnel, of a classic tale in which a short and pudgy hero trekked across unknown lands with the impossible goal of slaying a dragon. When he and his party reached the dragon's mountain, they camped in a corridor much like this one. The pudgy hero reminded him much of Chulii.

The corridor broadened a spell, and brightness came from faraway torches. Before he could really see much of anything, Maiman heard it: the collective cries of joy from a hundred little men, sing-song voices praising whatever gods or god their culture subscribed to. Whatever their religion, whatever its format, whatever hierarchy comprised it, whatever rituals it pertained, whatever history preceded it— he guessed that, at its head, sat a god of benevolence.

When he finally reached the spot where the Yesterlings gathered and exclaimed, Maiman almost dropped the still-warm remnant of his sword. The corridor walls of this section of Mount First, the section built by the Yesterlings themselves, caught the new light in a way he recognized but did not quite believe possible. It was a strange shine, an ermine white, moonlight cold, brilliantly opalescent shine. It was a shine that struck the eyes and made them look, froze the brain and made it gasp. His sword was crafted ages ago, back when silver ran aplenty; ran in molten rivulets down the forges and the ducts of Old Heth; paved the streets before and the pinnacles upon the keep so that moonlight made it shimmer, made it emanate, made the trifold splendor that every book of legend and myth always lauded— Maiman held his melted sword up to the walls and saw the legends reborn.

Maiman noticed scuffs, places where gilt was torn away, where fine decorum once sat splendid, where the hoards, the hoards the Yesterlings did not value as highly as their beloved ales, lay in heaping mounds. Most of it was gone. Most of it must have been gone, stripped away by the reitere. Even more of it was melted there, simply burned or torn to shreds. But still, there in the depths, Maiman saw the densest wealth he had ever seen or heard described. And the Yesterlings, the bumbling, go-lucky Yesterlings, the Yesterlings who swung no swords, forged no armor, fought no needless wars, had amassed it all. Piles of coins along the hallway, chests still overflowing with varied valuables, mosaics formed of raw gemstones inlaid in the walls.

Maiman fell to a knee then. Knight of Dreamtide, savior of Overtown, betrothed of Princess Galena, (former) bearer of the legendary blade Silvertongue, wept for the silly, jolly right folk; wept for their unfaltering trust, their innate taste of the wonderful, their inability to understand where that wonder is born. There is beauty in ignorance— there is sadness in knowledge. Something of value is lost when we overturn all rocks, when we evaluate every possibility. When gold's worth ceased to come from its glimmer and instead from its rarity, majesty shed a tear. Majesty died when we let that gold rot in vaults, when the streets became a threat to those who wore it on their necks and wrists.

Entire armies would lay down their lives, drench their pennants in blood, for a modicum of what these little men had reared in their home. Windows into antechambers were hewn of carefully cloven sheets of crystal, doors hung on hinges of polished cobalt and jade, torch sconces were cut from single formations of smoky white quartz. How deep, how much had these little men mined? How far had they surpassed those who came before them, the Huge Men? How many centuries had they labored here? Just for it all to be presented: not hidden behind ramparts and guarded by legions, not subject to a despot who claimed it all his own, not worshiped by enterprises or sleazy merchants, not funneled back into a nation's navy or otherwise injected into their war machine. It was all there, all shining and beautiful, just *because* it was all shining and beautiful.

And they went on. They walked down these corridors in echoing silence, a silence that spoke back to them, did not even detect the presence of the myriad little boots clanging on titanium floors or shuffling along emerald pathways. There were sections of great length, ones of startling width; off-shoot rooms where kings might once have sat, places where tremendous parties had been thrown, so many chambers where the drinks for those parties must be made, Hopshrooms still glowing with soft phosphorescence— but all remained silent.

It happened all at once. Maiman heard it and he saw it and he felt it in the same instant. The silence shouted, and so did the Yesterlings: they broke into their classic tumbling sprint and surged forth at once, crashed with jolly right happiness into one another as they ran. Out of the darkness came a matching wave of little men and women, shouting and greeting— and then embracing, and weeping. Maiman watched without moving, but the joy they felt was the same joy he felt. But his was pragmatic. His was laced with realization.

Chulii remained by Maiman's side, placed a hand upon his leg. "Why are you despondent, human?"

Maiman looked down, then back up at the walls, at the gold, at the silver. "All this . . . you cannot stay here, Chulii. We must leave soon, before the reitere return— the one we fought must have been left to guard what they found, but the others won't be long. It must have been . . . too much. They did not, could not know . . . that you had all this. They know now. They will not relent until all is gone."

Chulii nodded. "True enough, true as chuff. We will leave by morning."

Maiman looked at the group before him. The other wave of Yesterlings contained only a dozen or two.

"I have seen many battles, Chulii. But I still hoped that more of your people may have made it out," he said.

"So did I. But I suspected the truth, I did. Please do not fret, human— things are not as good as they could be if everything was good, but they *are* good. That is why I sent forward this other group, to see what had happened. That they survived their journey is gift enough. We sent them ahead, we did, because we could not risk putting all our eggplants in one barrel, you know? What if we had come altogether and met the Deer, eh? They made it by unscathed, but we did not.

"It was chance that let that happen. They might have gotten found, but they did not. Human, things are good. Now that we are whole again, we can start all over, dig out a new mountain in a new land. Others, many others might be gone, but they are always with us— here." The little man smiled his gap-toothed smile and tapped his temple. "We are Yesterlings, and we will make the damned best of things!"

Maiman laughed— a deep laugh that came from his whole body. He laughed so hard that tears came from his eyes. When he finally brought his head up, patted Chulii on the back, and looked forward again at the mass of jolly right Yesterlings twirling and dancing and stomping to unheard drinking songs, he already knew what he would see. He had felt it. Felt it the same way he felt the reitere when they passed in the woods, the same way he felt the Yesterlings' emotions, the same way he felt memories that were not his own. The stone he saw was sharp and silvery, laced with spots of brilliant gold, fixed with eyes the color of sunlight. He thought of the window and the backyard, of projectors and speakers and compasses.

But he thought mostly about her. Galena parted the sea of Yesterlings— and Maiman laughed once again. He laughed at the spinning of the little men, at the polite way they bowed and honored the royalty that was not their own, at their funny manner of speech as they saluted and praised, their over-exaggerated movements, the ways they showed their loyalty. Maiman laughed, because these little men, these strange but endearing little men, were far shrewder than they seemed.

Galena stopped a few feet from Maiman and smiled her silver smile.

"Now you are ready, my love," said Galena. Dancing motes of light popped into being around her, and her hair began to glow a soft scarlet or gold. "You have lived now. You have seen now. You have learned now. Now you can touch the threads which bind us all together, just as these folk have always done"

She stuck out her hand and smiled. "Dreamtide waits for us. I believe there has been quite a fuss since we left, with the future king and queen up and vanishing and all. Shall we return?"

Maiman smiled, but he did not reach out. An idea came to mind— this one was not inherited from anyone, but for once, forged in his own dull head. That didn't happen often. He turned to Chulii then, knelt before the little man so that their eyes were level.

Maiman reached out his hand. "Shall we?"

"Jolly right!" Chulii exclaimed and grabbed onto Maiman. A song went up among the Yesterlings as they crowded around, each hand grasping another's shoulder, until all in the tight space linked themselves together in an unbreakable chain.

A light flashed. Mount First, with all its silver and all its gold, would return to the earth. Reclaimed, as all things would be. *Almost* all things.

SHE WHO DESTROYS

Christine Boyer

Percy Mortimer wasn't a very good witch.

She wasn't even an *okay* witch. Both her mother and her grandmother were at least perfectly mediocre witches. All her ancestors, really, were good enough. They could perform easy enchantments or create simple charms. They weren't from a powerful bloodline. The Mortimer women had no Druid priestesses or oracles from antiquity in their lineage. They were, at best, working-class witches. The kind to set up shop at the edge of a village, to midwife mothers and babies, to barter tinctures for toothaches and the ague. The kind to scrape by, to make just enough to be comfortable. To have little in case they had to escape in the night lest the villagers blame them for some calamity.

They hadn't been forced to run for a long time (not since 1699, when Nehalennia Mortimer slipped the noose by transforming herself into a ribbon of fog, thus escaping a witchcraft charge of

107

driving two local men to madness). The Mortimer women had since lived in the same stone cottage for three hundred years—thirteen generations, with Percy being the thirteenth. It was almost a cliché, the bad luck of it. Born exactly three hundred years after her ancestor escaped death with a transformation spell, and Percy could barely conjure up a thread of smoke from a candle.

Her mother and grandmother ran a small shop in the town square—herbal remedies, curios, and soaps with a witchy slant for the occasional tourist. The shop did well enough to keep them housed and fed with a little left over, but its success was due to the older women.

Percy couldn't claim any of their success as her own. She lacked talent, and *talent* was just a different word for *patience*. The most important element of any spell was intention, of course, and Percy's intentions were always good . . . but execution counted too.

This left her a pretty bad witch, though a well-intentioned one. What she did have was *stubbornness*. She had it in spades. What she lacked in good witch-sense, she made up for in sheer pigheadedness, the intractability that made her dig in her heels, grit her teeth, and see a situation through to the bitter end.

Sometimes a witch needn't be very good. Sometimes all a witch needed was a similar tenacity to a mule.

Percy wasn't a very good witch, but she still went to the coven meetings each month with her mother and grandmother.

If she had been raised in a different sort of family, she would have marveled at how much her coven resembled an old ladies' church group—Bible study or altar committee. It had all the same hallmarks: metal folding chairs in a circle, a table bearing a carafe of coffee that tasted faintly burnt, day-old donuts cut into quarters.

Every new moon, they met in Brunhilda's finished basement to call the corners and work through an agenda that always bore the same complaints. The search for whoever sabotaged Estaria's garden with mint that ran rampant and choked out the other herbs. The plan for raising money to send someone over to England for the solstice celebration at Stonehenge ("Good networking opportunity!" proclaimed Ronna), though they never raised more than a few hundred dollars which inevitably ended up in the coffee-and-snacks budget.

Percy sat through it every month. She chewed on the same two quarters of donuts (one quarter of a glazed, one quarter chocolate iced). She drank the same water from her same bottle because the coffee, burnt and acrid, made her twitchy. She scuffed her sneakers against the carpet and listened to the women and waited for her turn.

"Any other business?" Ronna always chirped in the same bird-bright voice, and everyone's eyes swung over to Percy at the same time, as they always did.

And she always raised her hand (a holdover from school, though she was several years graduated now) and replied the same two words.

"Somerset Woods."

And the women of the coven heaved the same sigh every time.

Percy wasn't a very good witch, and sometimes she wondered if she wasn't very good at being a person, either. Everything always seemed so much more difficult for her.

School, for example. She had struggled to make friends and often stood off to the side during recess, unsure at how to join the games already in progress, the cliques already formed. She'd been lousy at kickball, hadn't seen the point of hopscotch. In high school, she was never invited to parties or weekend trips to the lake. She'd played no sports, joined no clubs.

The classroom had been worse. Math was a lost cause; the numbers never made sense. Why did it take a hundred cents to add to a dollar, for example, but only sixty seconds to add to a minute? How could fractions be numbers separated by both a line *and* a period? Why didn't someone just pick one and go with that? And why did it suddenly get so complicated with the addition of letters?

Reading was just the same. The letters didn't sit still for Percy the way they did for the other kids. Her letters squirmed and wiggled across the page, turning even simple reading exercises—*See the girl run! The girl runs fast!*—into an ordeal. Then came high school with required reading that made even less sense. Who was Dorothea Brook, for example, and why should Percy care about her marriage to some dusty old reverend?

The only place Percy had ever felt good was in Somerset Woods.

It only covered fifty acres, but it was plenty big to hold an entire world for a lonely little girl. Creeks and streams crisscrossed the woods and formed little valleys among the hillocks. The trees were thick with craggy bark, and their crowns kissed the blue sky. Percy had walked through Somerset Woods every afternoon, the shortcut between school and home. She was the only one—other kids said the woods were haunted, and they stuck to the safety of concrete sidewalks and yellow buses.

Somerset Woods had never felt haunted to Percy. She never felt an ounce of fear there, and even though it was a shortcut, she whiled away entire hours. She poked around the clay and mud of the stream banks. She lifted rotting logs and befriended the spotted salamanders who made the damp leaf-mold their home. She found interesting stones with flecks that sparkled, pocketed to line up on the windowsill of her bedroom.

She pretended she was a good witch. She snapped twigs and pretended they were wands, and it was a sort of magick in and of itself; how she could transform herself from a lonely, awkward girl into the queen witch of Somerset Woods. Numbers didn't confuse her there. Letters didn't crawl across the page and leap from the margin of her workbook. Kids didn't give each other sideways glances when she said something weird. She could be completely, entirely, just the Queen Witch of Somerset Woods.

She was only seven when the woods were taken from her.

"Perce—" her mother started, but Ronna held up her palm and silenced her. The same gesture each time. The *let's hear her out* gesture, even though they'd heard it a hundred times.

Each time, Percy promised that she would be level-headed, calm. She would be the adult she ostensibly was, even if she still felt like a kid most of the time.

"It's been fourteen years now," she started, as she always did.

Fourteen years since the developer came in and tore down the woods. Fourteen years since the streams and creeks were bulldozed under, the hillocks flattened, the salamanders ground into the mud. Somerset Woods was razed, stripped bare, and replaced with a grid of streets where each ended in a cul-de-sac. Houses sprouted like fat beige mushrooms after a rain. The frames went up, then the vinyl siding and windows, then the horrible bits and bobs that screamed faux fancy: columns and dormers and finials.

Thirteen years since the developer went bust along with the economy, leaving The Village at Somerset Woods a neighborhood of the dead. Half-built, the place had sat like a tumor at the edge of the village for over a decade.

No one had ever lived in the houses. Percy could have perhaps reconciled herself to the loss of the woods if those houses had been filled with life, with people living and fighting and loving each other. But to see Somerset Woods destroyed with nothing to show but a swath of crumbling beige homes?

"We didn't stop it when we had the chance," she continued, and that elicited the same grumbles of denial.

Which made her make the same accusations. They were a coven of witches with marginal power, and they did nothing with their collective talent aside from complain about invasive mint and raise money for trips that would never happen. It made the same hot flush of impotent rage course through her—how they hadn't lifted a single finger or wand fourteen years ago.

What would have been the harm to cast a spell, say, to delay the filing of permits? What would have been the harm to enchant the bulldozers and earthmovers to seize up their engines, to deflate their tires? If the developer was going to go bankrupt when the economy tanked, what would have been the harm to slow the destruction of the woods until the market crashed, as it was always going to do anyway?

Which made the other witches grumble more, the same defense that they couldn't change the course of history, that progress marched forward. That the law of three dictated their actions would boomerang back on them threefold, and who wanted to take that chance?

Which made Percy make the same plea she did each month for the past fourteen years.

"Wouldn't it be progress to destroy the development? It's already falling apart! Half of the houses have damaged roofs, and the sidewalks are already cracked, the lawns overgrown—"

Which brought the same admonishments—*we aren't a coven that destroys anything, put the thought out of your head immediately, young lady*—and which ended the meeting the same as it did every month.

Percy wasn't a very good witch, and maybe she wasn't a good person either because she dreamt of destroying that rotting neighborhood despite the coven's admonishments.

She thought of the cool clay between her toes on the stream bank. She thought of the salamanders with their friendly smiles and little feet, how they'd stretch out along her forefinger when she picked them up. She thought of the peace she felt in the woods, and then she felt rage at the loss of them.

She dreamt of drenching those empty homes in gasoline. She dreamt of dropping a match. Of the crackling as the fire consumed the cheap plywood and drywall, as it licked at the dead weeds that grew from the cracked sidewalks.

What made it worse was how the dreams didn't come at night when she slept: she forged them willingly during the day, thrilled at destruction she'd fashion if she had the chance. Then the daydream shifted to recreate the woods in her mind, to sculpt the flattened lands into the hills and valleys. She conjured the streams back into existence, restored the salamander families to their damp little homes.

Somerset Woods was always at the forefront of Percy's mind. At the family shop, while she restocked the shelves with blessed candles and new testers of oils. While she took the money from the till to the bank for the daily deposit. While she returned to the shop, only to see her mother and grandmother whispering then stop when she entered. The guilty way their gaze slid away from her was proof enough they'd been discussing her.

It was always her grandmother who knocked softly on Percy's bedroom door those nights, then stole inside to perch on the edge of her bed.

"I know you're angry," she always said, and she laid a cool palm to Percy's forehead, as if the rage could be tempered like a fever. "I know how angry this sort of helplessness can feel."

It was her mother, however, who thought busy hands quieted the mind, so she assigned chores that took entire weekends to complete. Like the weekend after their most recent coven meeting when she assigned Percy the task of cleaning out the basement of decades (centuries?) of detritus.

"Might as well put all that energy to use," her mother said.

Percy recognized a Grimoire when she saw one.

The Mortimer Spellbook sat on the kitchen shelf. It was stained from use, cracked in the spine, and loose pages fell out every time someone opened it. It held nothing nefarious—only incantations and recipes for healing, diagrams of herbs, and sketches of Moon in all her phases.

The book in her hands now was something else entirely.

She had no idea where it came from. She found it in the basement in a box of paperwork from the 1980's. It sat nestled on top of yellowed newspaper ("Ethical Tone 'Starts at the Top,' Dukakis Says") and underneath a recipe for spikenard oil. The Grimoire had no business being in such a mundane box, and yet there it was.

It was like it wanted to be found.

The cover was made of wood so old it was black with age, silky from centuries of handling. The pages inside were thick and not paper at all—they had the feel of some animal material, calf skin scraped and stretched.

The writing inside was like nothing Percy had ever seen before.

The ink might have been black when it was new, but it had faded over time to a dull iron color. The letters were jagged, thorny, and she blinked for a moment before she realized they weren't any letters she recognized. It wasn't the alphabet—the characters were slashes and spikes, drips of ink.

These characters didn't crawl off the page the way words usually did. They didn't wriggle into the margins like *See the girl! The girl runs fast!* did. The strange characters formed words that set on the vellum, solid as stones, and the more Percy stared at them, the more understanding began to settle over her.

Something unlocked inside her as she turned each page. She

took in the intricate diagrams, the lists of elements needed, the incantations. She felt, for the first time in fourteen years, the fiery rage in her cool by a degree.

The Grimoire wasn't a collection of spells like the Mortimer Spellbook. Each page was a detailed description of the steps needed for one single spell.

A Spelle to Invoke and Supplikate Kazamir

Percy knew the names of all the goddesses—Hekate, Ceridwen, Brigid. She knew the names of some intermediaries like Papa Legba. She didn't recognize the name Kazamir.

Perhaps he was a darker entity. She'd heard whisperings among the coven about certain demons and spirits. About the dark and dangerous magick they wielded.

And below it, in smaller script:

He Who Destroys

Patience didn't come easily to Percy, but stubbornness was second nature . . . and she found, with the Grimoire now in her possession, that stubbornness and patience could be kissing cousins in the right circumstances.

The spell to invoke Kazamir required thirteen elements times three—so thirty-nine. The math was so simple when she thought of it as thirteen plus thirteen plus thirteen, the numbers falling into order in a way they never had in school.

Thirty-nine things to gather from all five elements—air, water, earth, fire, and spirit. Percy consulted the Grimoire, ran her fingertip over the angry slashes of ink and felt the power transmitted from the page to her. It focused her impotent rage and gave it purpose.

It wasn't just the rage from the loss of Somerset Woods that burned hot and bright at the forefront of everything.

Rage from her lonely school years, her classmates who moved in circles of comradery and left her standing just outside, close enough to see but too far to join.

Rage from the numbers that made no sense, the letters that rearranged themselves until they were nonsense.

Rage from the coven and their inability to act on anything, how they wasted their collective power instead of trying to hold back the darkness that seemed to threaten the world.

Once Percy tapped into the boiling cauldron of anger underneath everything, it was easy to access. Comfortable to pull on and wear, like a soft, shapeless cardigan made cozy from age. It was easy to find more to be angry about.

She could see Somerset Woods as a single symptom to a larger sickness. The world had an insatiable need for more, for bigger, for newer. Instead of restoring the old homes in the village, why not destroy a lush piece of forest and trample it down? Instead of building well-made homes, why not slap them together fast and cheap so they lasted barely a decade before they started to crumble and rot? Why not squander the future for a cheap thrill in the present? Grind down the mountains, dig up the earth, tear up every plant by its root for cheap clothing, for a new phone every year, for a coffee machine that makes a single cup of coffee from plastic that will take generations to decay. Dirty up all the water. Poison the air. Push the other denizens of the planet into extinction and then create a word, *endling*, to describe the last of a species. Listen to the audio recording of the *Kauaʻi ʻōʻō* endling, the lonely mating call that would never be answered.

It was easy for Percy to hold the fury now, and Kazamir, when she summoned him, would help her hone it.

The first thirteen items were easy to gather. It was all water—the element of purification. Water was malleable. It took the shape of the vessel that held it. It could wear down mountains.

The thirteen elements: Dew gathered from the grass. Water from the placid face of a pond. Hail collected during a spring storm. River water, lake water, marsh water cloudy with algae.

Percy took a weekend to drive to the shore to collect brackish water where fresh met salt. She made war water, a glass from the tap mixed with rust and blessed with the words the Grimoire raised in her mind. She gathered fog, let it bead in the glass witch ball and distilled it into a few precious drops. Waterfall water. Water gathered from the rotted center of a stump.

She took an afternoon and went into the housing development. She never thought the woods haunted when she played there as a child, but the neighborhood was eerie. The houses stood empty but Percy's skin crawled as she walked through. The windows—those that hadn't been broken yet by bored teens from the village—were flat eyes that watched her as she searched for what she needed.

The twelfth item: water from The Village at Somerset Woods.

She found it eventually; there was a pile of abandoned construction materials, greyed two-by-fours under a faded tarp. The tarp made a small bowl between the gaps in the boards, and it held stagnant rainwater that squirmed with mosquito larvae.

Percy scooped it up into the glass jar then hurried home, her skin crawling at the gaze she felt on the back of her neck.

The thirteenth item was the easiest. Rage was so close to grief, and when she went to her room that night, she locked the door behind her and loosed her grief. She held the glass jar with the twelve other forms of water, and she let the salt of her tears bind them together.

The next thirteen items were also easy to gather. Percy was able to source most of them from the shop, though she had to dodge the watchful eyes of her mother and grandmother.

From its shelves, Percy collected: a freshwater pearl, a square of camphor, a conjure bag of Job's Tears. Polished jet. Henbane oil. An owl feather, the iridescent feather of a pigeon. A copper coin. A trio of cowrie shells threaded on a piece of hemp. Black salt. Dried rosebuds. Copal resin.

The thirteenth ingredient was the skull of a crow. Percy worried at her lower lip as she stood in front of the curio cabinet that held the shop's lone crow skull. It was easy to skim supplies from the top, but this was different. It might be noticed. Her grandmother kept a tight grip on the rare inventory.

She could have bought it outright, but it would have invited questions. They'd want to know what she was working on. They'd want to see the spellwork involved, the intended outcome.

Percy split the difference. The next morning, she opened the shop alone, and she placed her own money in the till. On the list where they kept track of who ordered what—important to ensure no one got into unintended shenanigans or dabbled in the darker arts—Percy put a fake name, noted a city two states over.

"We need a new crow's skull," her mother remarked that evening when they closed shop. "Looks like Perce sold it this morning."

"I'll add it to the list," her grandmother replied.

It was that simple.

The final thirteen items were trickier to pull together.

They were the binding elements of the spell, easily spoiled by impatience. Percy took a deep, steadying breath as she worked through the list. When the itch at the back of her skull threatened to make her rush the spell, she took a walk through the ruined homes that sat on top of the grave of her beloved woods. It replaced the itch with that cold-forged rage and reminded her of the purpose she now had.

She had to call Kazamir. She couldn't rush the spell.

She bought some items outright from the internet, depleting her meager savings on: an ornate scrying mirror, a jagged fulgurite formed when lightning struck a beach and fused sand together, a black opal that held a fiery universe in its center, and a bit of meteorite, a rock not of earth. She checked her email obsessively, tracked each parcel. She dashed home when each arrived, eager to intercept the delivery truck and head off any questions from her mother and grandmother.

Other things, she had to hunt on her own. The spell called for an iron nail from a house that burned down. Percy combed the local newspaper for house fires, and when it yielded nothing, she went to the library and went through back copies. She eventually found a story from five years back in a nearby town—an old

Victorian with faulty wiring. Percy did reconnaissance, drove past the site. A lucky break: the debris had been cleared away but the charred ground, overgrown with weeds, remained.

It took a nerve-wracking afternoon to find a nail. She rented a metal detector and swept the burnt-out lot. She felt exposed, felt eyes on her. She expected someone to call the police, to report the strange woman running a metal detector over land that didn't belong to her, but no one did. She left with a nail, bent and covered in soot.

It was far easier to find the tooth of a child. Her mother believed nefarious things could be done with the detritus shed from a body, so she'd saved all of Percy's milk teeth. Percy crept into her mother's room one afternoon and found the lacquered box that held her teeth. She selected a little molar.

It was also easy to create the cord woven from the hair of a witch. Percy figured she counted, even if she wasn't a very good one. She trimmed a strand from her head and studied the instructions in the Grimoire, the complicated nine-strand braiding.

Her fingers felt nimble. They flew as they plaited the cord, tight and smooth and beautiful. She'd never been good at braiding, her hands usually too clumsy to even braid the stalks of garlic that they hung over the doorway of their kitchen for good luck.

It was like she was being led. It felt like Kazamir was wide awake, standing just behind her and separated only by a thin veil between worlds. It felt like his hand guided hers: to braid this cord, to find that nail, to lift her milk-teeth in the lacquered box that rattled like dice.

What else did she need? A silken ribbon held up in a storm so that it was infused with the wild wind. Moss scraped from a grave on consecrated ground. She needed ashes from wood burned during the new moon, which meant she had to skip the monthly coven meeting for the first time ever. She gave a flimsy excuse ("headache") that seemed to fool neither her mother nor her grandmother.

"Are you sure it's just a headache?" her mother asked. She perched on the edge of the bed and pressed the back of her hand against her daughter's forehead. Percy could feel the gentle probing against her spirit, her mother seeking the truth behind the fib.

"I've just been tired lately," Percy amended, and that was closer to the truth. She *had* been sleeping poorly as she gathered the last thirteen elements. She dreamt of the blighted neighborhood as a beige tumor, a cancer that spread and consumed. She dreamt of it on fire, and then her dreams shifted to the memory of her woods, the scent of it in spring or summer or autumn.

She woke each morning before dawn with sweat prickling under her armpits. She woke breathless, her heart hammering against ribcage and never calming until she peered into the shadows of her bedroom and felt the presence that grew stronger with each ingredient she acquired.

"You need to sleep with a lepidolite under your pillow," her grandmother advised from the bedroom doorway. "Brings tranquility."

Percy nodded. "Sure. That's a good idea."

She didn't sleep that night at all, of course. It took forever to coax the wood to burn all the way through, then for the ashes to cool enough to bring home. Percy barely made it back to her room before her mother and grandmother returned from the coven meeting.

The eleventh and twelfth elements were symbols, so Percy chose the spot for her spell. She considered her bedroom first but immediately decided not to—for the same reason she rejected the shop. She'd been patient for the first time in her life, and she felt Kazamir's guiding hand, but she was not a very good witch. The likelihood that she had made a mistake was high.

Even when her rage burned at its hottest, Percy still loved her family more. She loved the women of the coven, even as they frustrated her with their inaction. She even loved the village and everyone who lived there, even if she felt separate from them and their lives. She wanted to perform the spell far away from everyone she loved in case the worst happened.

What better place than the blighted neighborhood then?

She spent an afternoon walking the grid of streets. She prowled each cul-de-sac and kicked the toe of her sneaker against the crumbling sidewalks. She let the presence of Kazamir guide her from where he stood just beyond the veil, and he led her to one home. There was a piece of plywood hammered over the front doorway. When Percy wriggled her fingertips underneath it, the nails gave out easily, like pulling rotting teeth from a jawbone.

Inside it reeked of mold and damp. The woods had smelled damp too, but it had been a good sort of rot: leaves turning to humus, mushrooms breaking down and feeding off stumps. It was like she'd been taught, the cycle of life and death and rebirth. Nothing really ended. Life always sprang from death. The phoenix always rose from the ashes. The serpent always ate its own tail.

Percy walked through the house that had never been a home.

She could picture it if she squinted, some family who would've hung pictures on the walls, set furniture in the rooms. They would have filled the place with life, and for the first time, the thought didn't raise anger so much as sorrow.

She chose the space that she assumed would have been the living room—a high-ceilinged room in the center of the house. She pulled the Grimoire out from the big pocket of her sweatshirt, and she turned to the page she needed. She studied the complicated symbol on the page, then reached into her pocket and pulled out the piece of chalk.

Within an hour, she had the eleventh element.

Then she reached into her pocket for the piece of charcoal and drew the same symbol in reverse: the twelfth element.

Percy stood back and admired her handiwork. The same symbol mirrored in black and white. All she had to do was bring everything the next night and then add the last element. After that, Kazamir would be summoned.

Percy wasn't a very good witch, but she knew her mother and grandmother. She knew when she'd been found out.

She'd felt their eyes on her for the past months. She'd seen them huddled together and whispering about her. Maybe she should have played it cooler, attended the coven meeting.

The knock on her bedroom door came just as Percy pulled on her sneakers. The sun was low in the western sky, steadily sinking towards the horizon, and she wanted to get to the abandoned house before nightfall. She had her sweatshirt on, and she had her backpack stocked with the remaining supplies: the prepared ingredients, the Grimoire, and a ceremonial tool she needed.

"Sweetie?" her mother called out, and that was the first clue they were trying to gently corral her. Her mother never used pet names.

The second clue: a second tap at the door, and then her grandmother's voice adding, "We made tea."

Percy could guess the tea she meant. They sold a blend at the shop, valerian and chamomile and more, for insomniacs. She knew it would make her eyelids turn heavy as stone. It would leave her insensate, while they would dig through her backpack and find the Grimoire. She couldn't let that happen.

There was no magick to locking the door with the old skeleton key, and it wasn't magick that made her kick at the key to snap it off in the lock. A second later, she heard her mother curse, heard the jiggle of the knob. Another second, and she heard them move towards the stairs back to the first floor.

She had no time now. Percy grabbed her backpack and pushed her window open. It was a short drop onto the soft ground, and she jumped without hesitation. Kept her knees bent and loose, rolled into the motion, and sprang up so smoothly that her high school gym teacher would have been amazed. Percy Mortimer, the girl who used to puke during the timed mile run in gym class: she sprinted now. Cut through the lawns of her neighbors, leapt over low fences. She raced against the sun, raced against her family looking for her, maybe even the other witches in the coven. Percy ran against everything except the purpose she'd honed over the past months, borne from the sorrow and grief of the past fourteen years.

See the girl run! The girl runs fast!

She reached the blighted neighborhood as if the wind hurried her along. She slowed to a quick walk, put her head on a swivel as she made her way to the house she had selected. She felt the usual gaze on her from the window-eyes of the empty buildings, but sensed nothing beyond that. No feeling of her mother or grandmother or other witches tracking her.

She knew it wouldn't last. She didn't have as much time as she wanted. She had to move fast.

The symbols she drew the day before were still there. Percy opened the Grimoire and studied the diagrams, then started placing the items. The child's tooth, the feathers, the stones . . . each one had its place. Her tongue formed the strange words without effort or thought. She was a conduit now, a live wire drawing the energy of Kazamir through the veil. The sprinkling of the thirteen waters. Blessing each cardinal direction, blessing above and below and beyond. Settling herself in the center of the symbols—the dark and the light both—Percy took a deep breath and pulled the athame out of her backpack.

The knife had been in her family forever. Maybe Nehalennia had used it, three hundred years and thirteen generations ago. Who could say? It felt fitting, though, to use it now for the last element of the summoning spell.

A person's life blood.

Percy had whetted the knife to a wicked sharpness. It wouldn't do to mess the spell up at the last minute by botching the cut. It had to be quick, though it wouldn't be painless, because pain was how Kazamir tore through the veil between his world and hers.

Another deep breath. Another and another until her hand steadied. She thought of the damp-smelling house she knelt in now and felt the familiar rage, but as she lifted the knife to her own throat, as her blood splashed hot and coppery on the chalk and charcoal symbols, her thoughts veered to the memory of Somerset Woods and the peace she felt there.

Her life faded with each faltering beat of her heart. The veil tore to admit Kazamir to her world. Percy died with the memory of a little spotted salamander in her hand, the sunlight dappling through the filigreed crowns of the trees.

Percy wasn't a very good witch, and she often felt that she wasn't a good person, but she should have never worried as much as she did.

Of course she was a good person. Good people feel anger and rage and grief, and hers had always been centered around the destruction of the peaceful green place that felt like home. Her anger and grief may have burned hot at the surface of her, but if she'd dug deeper, she would have found the true wellspring of her emotions was love.

Kazamir knew. Little was hidden from him. The veil was a pane of clear glass, and it allowed him to see the hurt, lonely witch who worked so hard to summon him. When he stepped into Percy's world from his own, he already knew the real intentions of her heart—and hadn't Percy's mother always taught her that intention was the most important part of any spell?

Nothing really ended. Life always sprang from death. The phoenix always rose from the ashes. The serpent always ate its own tail.

The first thing Kazamir did was reach down and touch the tip of his finger to Percy's forehead. He pushed the spark of life back into her and watched as it settled and bloomed like a wildflower in spring.

The second thing Kazamir did was grant Percy's wish . . . kinda.

There was destruction, and there was unmaking. To destroy was to annihilate, to be reckless and leave a swath of debris in one's wake. To destroy the blighted neighborhood was to leave smoldering ruins, charred framework, cracked and pitted sidewalks and driveways.

To unmake, though?

He knew what stood here before. The young witch's mind held every stream and rise of earth, every hidden spring, every tree and gnarl of wild grapevine, every acorn sprouting in the moss on the forest floor, every chipmunk and squirrel, every chirping bird. Every beloved salamander.

The young witch's heart held her true wish. She didn't want to burn or destroy. She wanted to restore. How many times had she dreamed of destruction, but had her mind slip to imagining the woods returned to their glory?

Kazamir was neither good nor bad—he only bent to the will of the one who summoned him. Percy was a good person, even a great person, and her love always outshone her hate. He Who Destroys found himself as He Who Unmakes, and he unmade the blighted neighborhood.

The faux-fancy elements of the homes disappeared. The houses were unconstructed into their composite parts. The drywall broke into gypsum and paper; the latter returned to the pulped tree it came from, the former returned to the earth. The wood frames disappeared and trees all the way out west in Oregon reappeared where they once stood. The glass windows returned to sand, dolomite, limestone, sank back to their source.

Once the homes were gone, the flat lots were unmade. The earth heaved and pitched, reformed its natural contours. The streams and creeks burbled from the ground and reshaped their banks and pools. The trees grew from seeds to saplings to towering giants in seconds. The ferns unfurled; the moss spread. The entire unmaking happened in utter silence until the first mourning dove cooed and signaled the return of Somerset Woods.

That is where Percy wakes. She wakes to moonlight and the song of nightbirds, the gentle sound of water burbling over rounded stones.

She sits up and touches her throat. She'll see the scar once she's in stronger light, the thin white line where she had sacrificed her life blood to restore a bit of the world to itself. It will be a reminder of the cost of magick, and she'll bear it gladly for the rest of her long life.

The Grimoire will never be found again in her lifetime. She will always believe it wanted to be found. Perhaps Kazamir took it with him to keep safe until another not very good witch should have need for it.

The book isn't the only thing missing. The unmaking was not just physical: the entire existence of the blighted development has been unmade from memory. Articles have disappeared from old newspapers. The developer will have gone bankrupt a few months sooner, and everyone will have forgotten the splintered bit of an alternate reality.

Indeed, when her mother and grandmother find her—the rest of the coven at their heels—they will stop in their tracks, suddenly puzzled as to why they are rushing to find her in the first place. Why are they so worried? Percy is a good witch and a better person, and everyone knows she is the Queen Witch of Somerset Woods.

DANDELION WISHES

Leora Spitzer

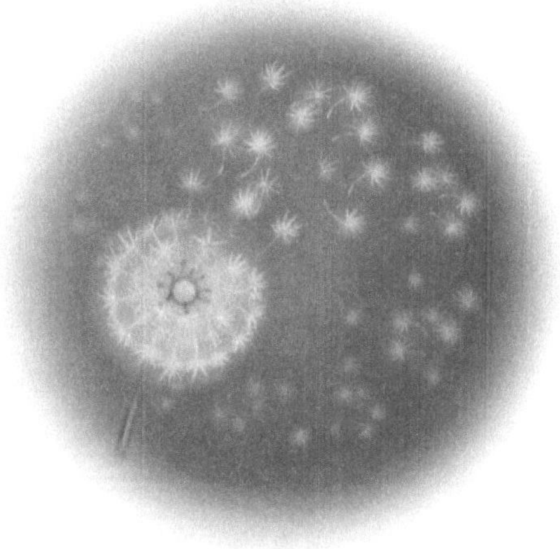

Dafna leaned her head back against the tree, letting her pencil fall to the ground. Sweat was beginning to pool between her breasts, and the tickle of grass against her calves was turning into more of an itch. Soon, it would be time to go home, back into the cool air conditioning, but right now standing up felt like a bigger chore than staying out in the heat. Absently, she plucked a silver dandelion and pursed her lips, considering. *I wish I had someone to talk to,* she thought, blowing the seeds into the wind, and then a moment later: *I wish I believed there was any point in making wishes.*

"Of course there's a point," someone said. Dafna jerked, bumping her head on the rough bark. She had been quite sure she was alone in the little park. All of the neighbors who'd walked by had been thoroughly focused on their own lives. No one had even glanced in her direction, let alone entered the park.

131

And then, of course, there was the minor detail that the voice had responded to her thoughts. While Dafna did frequently mutter to herself when she was alone, she was reasonably sure that this time she had not spoken aloud.

A quick glance confirmed that there was no one else in sight. She shook her head firmly, wondering if she had gotten too much sun, and took a long drink from her water bottle. "When in doubt, hydrate" had been one of her mother's favorite precepts, and it was honestly annoying how often it proved to help.

Not this time, though. As soon as she had recapped the bottle, the voice said, "On the other hand, there's no point in wishing for someone to talk to if you won't talk, you know."

Dafna swallowed, squeezing the water bottle like it might be able to protect her. "I don't like talking to people when I have no idea who or where they are."

"I'm the dandelion spirit, of course," said the voice impatiently. And then she was there.

If Dafna had been asked to imagine what a dandelion spirit would look like, she would have drawn someone tiny and slender like a dandelion stalk, with wispy silver clothes and hair. Instead, the spirit was as round and cheerful as the dandelion blooms. She did seem a little wispy around the edges, like an Impressionist figure in an otherwise-Realist painting, but she occupied the space of a person sized and shaped very much like Dafna herself—far more alike than Dafna would have imagined. None of the fairies in picture books or movies were fat, but apparently that had more to do with the biases of the illustrators than the body types of ethereal beings.

If this was real.

"The dandelion spirit?" Dafna repeated. If this was just a weird dream, she hoped it lasted. Her dreams lately had been filled with more storms than sunlight, and she could use a bit of whimsy.

"Well, sure," the spirit said, sitting in the grass beside her. There was a faint greenish tinge to her skin, and her windswept curls were a vibrant yellow. She wore a dress made of thousands of tiny petals, a braided flower crown, and silver dandelion fluff earrings that dangled from her slightly pointed ears. "When you make a wish on a dandelion seed, it doesn't just happen, you know. Someone has to make it happen." A wide grin stretched across her plump cheeks, and Dafna felt an answering smile blossom involuntarily on her own face.

She thought of other wishes she'd made on dandelion seeds over the years—charming childhood requests, but also teenage wishes that were mortifying in retrospect, and a few deeply intimate wishes that she never would have made if she had known someone was listening—and the smile froze in place. "Do you respond to all dandelion wishes?" she asked apprehensively.

"Well, not all," the spirit said, stretching out in a sunbeam like a cat. Dafna, who was used to trying to make herself smaller around other people, to take up less space, watched enviously—though admittedly her gaze was caught as much by the tantalizing hint of the spirit's ample cleavage as it was by the unapologetic way she carried herself. "Just in this neighborhood. Anything larger would be unmanageable."

Dafna relaxed. She'd lived in a different city as a teen, so if someone had been listening, at least it was not someone she was currently expected to speak to. "You actually make wishes come true?" she asked.

The spirit shrugged. Dafna's eyes followed the curve of her shoulder, the sunlight glowing against her skin. "Only the little wishes," she admitted freely. "World peace is rather out of my capacity, for example."

"What kind of wishes, then?"

She grew serious, running a narrow furrow into the soil with a finger. "The most important wish is the wish of the flowers, but that's always the same: that their seeds find a good safe place to land and grow. But after that, I do my best with the humans' wishes. After all, they help me fulfill the flowers' wish, so it's only fair."

"That makes sense," Dafna agreed. "What kind of human wishes do you grant, if not world peace?"

This time, her grin was conspiratorial. "You know that little boy who lives in the blue house?"

Dafna nodded. She had never officially met the boy, but she had heard his dads calling, "Max! Don't climb the neighbor's tree!" or "Max, if you poke the roses, they will poke you back!" or "Max! No running in the street!"

To the spirit, she said, "You mean Max?"

"Yes, him. He wished for ice cream the other day, so I whispered to the ice cream man that it might be a good idea to drive down his street, and between the hot sun and Max's excitement when he heard the music, it didn't take his dads very long to agree to a treat."

Dafna grinned, remembering the joy of licking melted ice cream off her fingers on a sweltering summer day while the truck's tinny music faded into the distance. "Well done," she said.

The spirit glowed. Literally. "Why, thank you, I was quite

pleased with myself for that one," she said with no trace of modesty. It was the kind of response that would have irritated Dafna's mother, but Dafna wished she could accept compliments on her work with that kind of poise, without always assuming the complimenter was just being kind or polite rather than genuine, allowing herself to admit to taking pride in her accomplishments.

"What else?" she asked.

The spirit hummed, a sound rather like the crickets who sang in the park at night. "The old man in the house with the big porch swing wished that his roses would grow as well as the dandelions did," she said. Dafna knew that Mr. Williams was not actually that old, but she also had the sense that he'd been waiting his whole life to be a crotchety old man puttering around in the garden yelling at people to get off his lawn, so she let it go.

"Can you make roses grow?" she asked instead.

"No one can make roses do anything they don't want," the spirit said. "They have to be flattered. But I was pleased that he'd noticed the good work I was doing with the dandelions, so I made the effort. It turned out they really wanted to be able to climb, so I gave the old man a dream about a garden full of trellises, and eventually, he gave it a try. They're all much happier now."

Now that Dafna was thinking about it, she did vaguely recall seeing Mr. Williams building trellises earlier in the summer, and his roses were quite beautiful. She'd seen Max's harried dads chase him out of Mr. Williams' yard more than once.

"I'm sure he was very grateful," she said, deciding not to tell the spirit that Mr. Williams' comment about the dandelions had most certainly not been intended as a compliment, even if he had been dispersing dandelion fluff at the time.

"Well, he took all the credit for his genius, of course, but I know what I did and that's enough for me," the spirit said, her curls bobbing gently in the wind. She looked at Dafna thoughtfully. "Want to hear another one?"

"Yes, please."

The spirit pointed across the park. "You know the woman who lives in that house?"

Dafna stilled. She didn't know Eden Silverberg, not really. They had only spoken briefly, in passing. But she had noticed the single mother in synagogue, on the street, and in the supermarket, spotted the little bi pride flag pin she wore, seen the tender look she gave her toddler even when the child was screaming. Of all the intriguing glimpses Dafna had gotten into the other woman's life, it was the wrinkle of familiar anxiety in her forehead that most suggested they might be able to understand each other deeply and that kept her from approaching, not wanting to demand any attention from someone who clearly had a full plate.

The dandelion spirit was still looking at Dafna expectantly. "Yeah," she said. "I know her."

"Well, she has this rock," the spirit said. "A river-smoothed stone that fits in her palm. She calls it her worry-rock and carries it around in her pocket, and whenever she's anxious, she turns it over in her hand a few times. It helps calm her down."

This one felt more personal than the other stories, and Dafna felt that she ought to stop the spirit, ought to refuse to intrude on Eden's privacy, but she could not bring herself to form the words.

"Anyway, she lost the rock for a while, and it was stressing her out. In a fit of whimsy, she made a wish to find it, even though she doesn't believe in dandelion wishes and thinks she ought not to believe in the worry-rock's power. But I found the rock very easily since it was awfully worried about being away from her. I managed to get the curtains at just the right angle at just the right time that a sunbeam lit up the spot under the counter where it had fallen, and she found it right away."

Dafna pictured Eden's relief, the tension slipping away from her shoulders as she scooped up the stone. Not for the first time, the artist found herself wishing that she could be the one to soothe the other woman's anxiety. She said, somewhat hoarsely, "I'm glad you were able to help her."

"Me too," the spirit said, twirling a dandelion stalk between her fingers. Dafna had not seen her pick it. She held it out to the artist with a half-smile full of summer sunshine and the scent of warm earth. "One more?" she offered.

Dafna accepted the flower. She looked again at the spirit, closed her eyes, and blew. A moment later, she heard the rustle of wind through the grass. "You're doing just fine on your own, honey," the spirit whispered into her ear, and pressed a firm kiss onto her cheek.

When she opened her eyes, she was alone with the flowers. There was no trace of the spirit—even the blades of grass where she had been sitting stood tall. Dafna took another sip of water. Most likely she had fallen asleep and her subconscious had, for once, decided to give her something sweet.

She looked down at her sketchpad, brushed dandelion seeds off the page, and bit her lip, considering. She picked up the pencil.

Eden sat at the kitchen table, enjoying the quiet. Aaron had finally fallen asleep, and she knew she ought to use the break to pick up the toys he'd left all over the floor, or maybe wash the lunch dishes, but surely it would be okay to just sit and breathe for a moment.

Then, someone knocked lightly on the door. Eden briefly considered ignoring it, hoping they would go away—but what if the visitor started knocking more loudly, or worse, rang the door-bell? She didn't want to risk waking Aaron, not when he'd been so cranky and desperate for his nap, so she pulled herself up out of the chair and hurried to the front door.

To her surprise, Dafna Shapiro stood on the stoop, smiling a little awkwardly and clutching a large sketchbook to her chest. Eden didn't really know her, not in a way that mattered, but she knew of her. The large painting of the burning bush in the shul atrium that Eden regularly paused to admire was Dafna's work. She'd thought about approaching the artist, but, well, Aaron was always demanding her attention, and what would she have to say to someone so talented, anyway?

"I'm sorry to bother you," Dafna said. She jerked her head toward the little park across the street. "I hope this isn't too weird, but I've been sketching over there all morning, and I thought maybe you'd want this one." She pulled a sheet of paper from the sketchbook and handed it to Eden, not meeting her eyes.

It was drawn from the point of view of a ladybug or some other small creature close to the ground. Large, out-of-focus dandelions loomed in the foreground, leading the eye to the central image: a detailed and intricate rendering of Eden's home. Dafna had even drawn the menorah that Eden had neglected to move from the windowsill in the months since Hanukkah had ended.

The enormous plants lent a certain magical whimsy to the little house, which, in Dafna's eye, looked warm and welcoming rather than the cluttered mess Eden knew it to be.

"Thank you so much," Eden said, tracing the lines with a light finger. "It's beautiful."

"Oh, no trouble," Dafna muttered. Just when Eden thought she was going to need to repeat the compliment, the artist squared her shoulders and looked up, unfolding her arms and letting the sketchbook fall to her side to reveal soft curves that Eden longed to sink into. "I mean, thank you," she said clearly, smiling shyly. She had adorable dimples that Eden had never noticed before, and there was a smudge on her cheek, almost shimmering where the light hit it. The color and shape reminded her of how she and her friends used to paint each other's skin with dandelions when she was a girl, or maybe of a lipstick stain from someone wearing an unusual shade. But there was a much more obvious explanation for an artist.

"Were you painting this morning?" she blurted. Dafna blinked, confused. "Just … you've got a bit of yellow on your cheek, right here." She touched her own cheek on the spot. Dafna mirrored the gesture, surprise and an unaccountable wonder dawning in her deep brown eyes. Eden felt herself begin to flush.

"Come in," she urged. "If there's one thing that I have plenty of, it's wet wipes—you would not believe how sticky Aaron gets. And it's been so hot out—I'll get you some water, or lemonade if you'd prefer." She waved off the other woman's instinctive demurral. "Really, it's the least I can do after you gave me this lovely work of art."

"It's just a sketch," Dafna protested as she followed Eden into the house. Eden closed the door behind her, looking again at the details in the drawing. She felt suddenly lighter, like a dandelion fluff floating on the wind, sure to find a bit of fertile earth in which to plant itself. Holding the paper as tenderly as a fragile seed, she went to welcome the artist into her home.

IT'S NOT REALLY ABOUT JACK

Andrea Chesman

Clangsy banged into the kitchen and planted herself—magnificent as a blue spruce—near her husband. "What is got into you? The hay no cut itself and rain do come anytime soon. Go!"

"Come," Garwin barked, never one to use two words when one would do. He held his meaty arm out to her. Though he was equally magnificent in stature, there was a gentleness to his gestures. She drew near so he could wrap his arm around her substantial waist and rest his head against her soft belly, as needy as a child.

"Oh, darlin'," she said, gentling her voice and stroking the tangled brown hair that held a few silver threads. "Sick are ya? I no ever seen ya like this."

"'Tis the nightmares," he said. "I seen my future and 'tis bad, Clangsy. A Measly man will be the death of me."

"You still on about that?" She pushed herself free and thumped over to the sink where she began to swipe at the breakfast dishes with a wet rag. "I no can believe you let that fortune teller get you so up riled. No one knows futures. Not some flouncy with a velvety hat on her head." She scrubbed fiercely. "And you so big and strong." She was not flattering him. Garwin's size and strength were legendary. "There be no Measly what can bring you down."

"No, Clangsy, you be wrong. There is Measly trouble ahead. I do feel it in my bones." He sighed, his breath redolent of egg and onion, ruffling the curtains. "But you have some rightness—the hay do no cut itself." He creaked his bones upward and shuffled toward the door, where he paused and said, "But Clangsy, will ya say to me if any beanstarks pop up in the garden where they no belong? Will ya just do that for me?"

"'Course I will," she said grudgingly over her shoulder. But as she continued to wash the dishes, she muttered to herself, "Beanstarks in the garden! There's all the time beanstarks in the garden. What does he think we et?"

Clangsy went about her chores—it was a wash day—and she brooded. If the fortune teller really could see the future, what was hers? Wasn't she supposed to spend her whole life with Garwin, the big lug. Why did he go to that fortune teller? Why look for trouble? Trouble comes, trouble goes, we all the time meet trouble.

After she finished pegging the laundry to the line, she trudged over to her best friend's house for a visit. Clangsy found Bangor gathering mushrooms in the woods. "You ever seen a Measly?" Clangsy asked.

"Hello to you, too."

"Sorry. Hello. I got a lot on my head."

"Meaning your grumbly, rumbly humbly?"

"Maybe."

"Why?"

"That fortune teller at the fair is so why. She say Garwin will die at the hand of a Measly man, so he be on the look-out. As though a teensy wee folk could hurt such a big one like his self."

"Knucklehead!" said Bangor, never one to hold back.

"No knucklehead! No say that!"

"Suit you self. I knows a knucklehead when I see one." Bangor shrugged and turned back to her gathering, letting Clangsy leave in a huff. Because they were best of friends, they got on each other's nerves all the time.

Clangsy returned home and got the wood stove raging. She sliced a thick steak from a hanging leg in the cold house, and set it in a pot on the stove. She peeled and chopped a mountain of root vegetables and potatoes and soon she had a big stash cooking, giving off a tantalizing aroma. After a while she heard the distant rumbling that heralded Garwin's approach.

Oh my, she thought, I can hear Garwin's belly growling from here. He's hungry, that's for sure. Soon, in addition to Garwin's stomach grumbles, she could hear his footsteps pounding closer and closer. But instead of bursting through the door as usual, he stopped right at the threshold and sniffed loudly. Then he bellowed, "Fee, fi, fo, fum, I smell the blood of a foolish knave. Be he scared or be he brave, I'll pound his bones to make his grave." He looked all around the cottage but couldn't find the source of the smell. "Wife! Was there a Measly man here?"

"'Course not, Garwin. You just smell my good stewstash. Come put your face in my supper." As she spoke, she placed two large bowls, then a pitcher of ale, a loaf of bread, and two mugs on the table.

Garwin set himself down heavily and began to spear morsels of meat with his knife, mopping huge hunks of bread in the gravy. Clangsy tried to make conversation, commenting on the upcoming harvest festival. Garwin merely grunted, attending to his business at hand. She asked if he thought the weather would hold until he got the last of the grasstarks in the barn. "Blagh," Garwin answered, with a mouthful of rutabaga. Clangsy sighed and took her plate to the sink.

"Cake?" asked Garwin after a belch loud enough to rattle the mugs on the wall.

"No cake. Pie. Rambleberry pie."

Garwin dispatched his dessert with great enthusiasm, berries slipping into his beard for his later enjoyment. He stood and rubbed up against Clangsy. "Leave dishes now?" He grinned and waggled his butt at her, a display she was supposed to find appealing.

"I no can leave dishes. I no can leave weaving. You need a warm coat for winter." She pushed him aside. "Go smoke a pipe and leave me to peace."

Clangsy's loom was set up in the room that was supposed to be the nursery, but no babies ever came to fill it. Instead there was a goose, Garwin's singing harp, and a dollhouse Clangsy once played with. She sat herself down at her loom, but as she started to send the shuttle flying, the goose began to head butt her backside while the harp snickered malevolently. Clangsy batted the goose away. The goose nipped her, hard.

"What got yous so up riled?" Clangsy turned from the loom. "Settle down or I will—"

"You will what?" asked the harp. "Sic the Measly man on us?"

"No Measly man here, Plucky. So shut it. I will chop you to firewood."

"Is too a Measly. Check the dollhouse."

"Is not."

This went on for a while, with Goldy still nipping. Finally, Clangsy heaved herself up from her bench and went over to the dollhouse. She lifted off the roof and peering down said, "There be no—"

But there was. There was a Measly man, lying on a feather bed, head propped up with his arms crossed behind his head, looking up at Clangsy for all the world like the happiest creature who lived. She stared down at him in horror; he looked up at her and smiled. Neither moved for a moment. Then Clangsy replaced the roof and left the room.

The next morning, as soon as Garwin left for the fields, Clangsy returned to the dollhouse. She reached into the house and plucked the little guy up from the kitchen where he stood. "What is you doing here?"

"Hiya," said the Measly man. "Pleased to meet you, your Largeness."

"What you doing here?"

"Just resting. Got anything to eat? I am feeling a bit peckish." At that, the goose honked loudly.

Without thinking, Clangsy started to set him down. "I'll get you some eatings." She was that thoughtlessly welcoming.

"Wait! Please don't go. How did you grow to be so big? Are you an angel? Am I in heaven?"

"I know not this Heaven country you speak of," said Clangsy. "And I know not what are angels."

The Measly man broke out in a big grin. "Phew!" he said. "Good thing! Means I'm not dead yet."

"Dead man, dead man, dollhouse resting. You be a dead man, when Garwin finds you nesting," sang the harp, and the goose honked her agreement.

"Indeed," said Clangsy. "Iffen you see my man, you make yourself small."

"I am small. Is he big like you?"

"Bigger. Biggest."

"And he hates Measlies," said the harp with a malicious chuckle.

"Am I a Measly?"

"So you are," said Clangsy. "What do you call yous self?"

"I call myself Jack. I'm a man, a human man. And you must be a Giant . . . err . . . Giantess."

"Well, Jack Man. Giants no like human mans."

"Well, Your Gracious Giantess, to tell ya the truth, Giants have a bad reputation down below. They are known to smash everything to smithereens."

"What is smithereens?"

Jack thought for a minute, glancing around the room as if looking for a clue. "Darned if I know, Your Greatness."

"Well, my Garwin no never has gone down below, so no smithereens from him. And call me Clangsy. I be back with fresh food later, after chores."

"Take me with you. We can visit while you work."

Clangsy liked the idea of company while she worked, so she

slipped Jack into her apron pocket, curious to hear more from him. As Clangsy attempted to have a normal day of cleaning and cooking and gardening, Jack, secure in her pocket, called forth a steady stream of questions, like *why does the harp sing* and *can the goose talk?*

No one had ever shown such an interest in Clangsy. Mostly she spent her days alone with her thoughts—and her grievances—but here was Jack, complimenting her on her garden and trying to help her harvest rasperberries, though he fell out of her pocket a few times.

Down below, Giants have a reputation as being slow-witted and quick to anger, but in truth, Giants have a wide range of personality traits, just like humans. Clangsy, like Jack in a way, was curious. So she had plenty of questions for Jack, too, including how he got to her home.

"'Twas strange," he told her. "I was leading a half-dead cow to market, when this man comes out of nowhere and offers to trade me some magic beans for ol' Katinka. 'Course I made the trade 'cause Katinka was nothin' but a bag of bones with udders. My wife was awful mad, and she threw me and the beans outta the house. Like magic then, those beans grew so tall they went right through the clouds. So I says to myself, wonder what's up there. I decided to climb up that beanstalk and see what's what. I didn't know when I stepped offen the vine would I fall through the clouds or not. But the beans brought me right to you. Is that magic or what?"

Clangsy was flattered, and charmed. Jack had just said more words than Garwin said in a week, a month. And the words kept tumbling out of Jack's mouth, how he was meant to be a guy who didn't worry about the small things—like bringing home the bacon. He lived to drink and dance and sing. He told her he was a big-picture guy, though none of his big-picture plans had worked out. So far. But they would. (Clangsy had no idea what a big-picture guy was. Someone who painted murals?)

With Jack in her pocket, every day was a new adventure for Clangsy. Tiny Jack navigated her world in ways she never imagined. He could thread a darning needle faster than she. When there was dusting to do, Jack put one foot on a dust rag and pushed off with the other foot, skating around the knick-knacks until the bare wood shone. In the kitchen, Jack slid down her arm and rolled over and over on the biscuit dough as though he could replace a rolling pin. (He could not.) When she churned butter, he danced a jig, keeping time with the beat of the paddles. And he sang. He knew songs, beautiful songs that stood the hair up on the back of Clangsy's neck.

Each day when Clangsy heard Garwin's thunderous footsteps signaling his return home and the need to hide Jack in the dollhouse, Jack said to her, "Maybe it's raining, maybe it's pouring, maybe you just heard the old man's snoring."

The first time he said that, she protested. "No, 'tis him. I knows it."

Jack smiled. "Yeah, I know. I made a joke." Whenever Clangsy didn't understand Jack's point, he told her it was just a joke. Since the Giants of Cloud Country were not big on comedy, Jack's idea of a joke was beyond Clangsy's understanding.

Meanwhile, Garwin's daily threats to the Measly he smelled were getting tiresome. Each evening when he returned to the house, he bellowed some variation or another of "Fee Fi Fo Fum." The one that particularly irked Clangsy was "I smell the blood of a Measly man. Be he live or be he dead, I'll grind his bones to make my bread," since she was the sole wheat grinder and bread maker. But when the harp took to teaching Garwin new ones—like "Eeeny, meany, miney mo. Catch a Measly by the toe. When he hollers, let him know, how you kill a Measly foe"—Clangsy found it even more annoying.

In truth, the singing harp Garwin bought with their hard-earned savings always annoyed Clangsy, and she hadn't found much in Garwin to appreciate for a long time. One stillbirth and three miscarriages sucked much of the hope out of their union. Although she was well aware of the unlikelihood of carrying a baby to term—babies were few and far between in Cloud Country—she took the end of each pregnancy hard and started spending more and more time weaving in the evening, letting Garwin fall asleep first, often with the harp in his arms, a weirdness Clangsy chose not to examine too closely.

There was much she chose not to examine, including Jack's story about climbing a beanstalk. She didn't think a "beanstalk" was the same as a "beanstark" though Jack's dialect seemed so close to the language she and Garwin spoke that she should have noticed. After Clangsy told Jack that sometimes the goose laid a golden egg, she chose to ignore Jack's excitement about golden eggs and instead remarked about the gamey quality of a goose egg and promised him a bit of omelet. When Jack asked about the fine feather beds and velvet curtains in the beautifully appointed doll-house, she was happy to talk about decorating and didn't register Jack's interest as greed.

One day, Jack tried to wiggle his way down into the slot of Garwin's piggy bank to retrieve a coin that Garwin had put there after selling a golden goose egg. Clangsy watched him struggle, wondering what he would do with the coin since she provided everything a Measly could want: a home and good food—and good company. It was all *she'd* ever wanted.

Considering how fat he had become on Clangsy's cooking and how small the slot was where the coins were deposited, Jack's attempt to break into the bank was ridiculous, even laughable. Sure enough the harp began to laugh. "Jack, Jack, you can't win. You're too fat to get out, if you ever get in." The goose added a few honks and slapped her webbed feet in a show of hilarity, and even Clangsy had to stifle a giggle. She gently pulled Jack from the piggy bank slot where he was stuck—butt over better sense—and put him in her pocket. Jack sulked in her pocket for the rest of the morning. Neither said anything about the fact that Jack was attempting to steal a coin.

One day, Jack declined Clangsy's invitation to sit in her pocket, saying he had a stomachache. Was it the goose egg omelet she gave him? Or perhaps a bit of meat was off? Garwin and Clangsy— indeed all the Giants—had cast-iron stomachs that were hard to upset. But maybe the same food wasn't good for a Measly. She had a bad feeling about this and decided to seek the advice of Bangor.

Bangor had no sympathy for Jack's discomfort. "He is just belly-aching I bet."

"Well, that's what I said," said Clangsy, puzzled.

"I mean he has homesick pain. Send him home."

"No! Not ever will I. I think . . . I think I love him."

Bangor snorted. "Is not love. Is fun. Is entertainment. Dose him with mint and chamomile tea. And quit the belly-aching, that's what I say. To the both of yous."

Clangsy didn't think Bangor had gotten to the root of the problem. "But what about—"

"What about nothing? No cure for you. Too much foolishness all around." Bangor turned away, and Clangsy left without saying good-bye.

Anger carried Clangsy for a while. Bangor didn't understand Jack; she didn't understand Clangsy; she didn't know what it was like to live with Garwin. Still, Clangsy followed Bangor's advice and stopped in a meadow near her house to gather mint and chamomile flowers for tea. She had just filled her apron when she heard a piercing high sound, like a whistle, like a song. It was the harp, sounding an alarm. Heading toward the sound, she heard the harp singing in its shrillest voice, "Garwin, Garwin, for sooth, for sooth. A Measly man is stealing your goose." Would the voice carry into the forest where Garwin was chopping wood? She heard clearly, "The goose is noosed; a Measly man is stealing the goose."

Clangsy dropped her apron, spilling the herbs she had collected, and started running home. As she ran she heard a loud crash of metal on rock telling her Garwin had thrown down his axe. Next came a thunderous roar of outrage, sending the leaves quivering on the trees. His footsteps pounded as he pushed trees from his path, crashing, smashing, booming. His fury filled the air. Garwin ran so fast his footfalls became a continuous roar of thunder. Could Jack possibly outrun a raging Giant? Still the harp sang, "Garwin, Garwin. Blame your wife. She harbors Jack to ruin your life."

"No!" shouted Clangsy. "There is no truth there!"

Just as she arrived in the garden, there was Jack, riding the back of the goose and reaching for a particularly tall and sturdy beanstalk. "Jack!" she called out, her voice pleading, for what she did not know. He never even glanced back. That ungrateful thief never gave Clangsy a thought.

Garwin smashed through the garden gate, his face red, his fists clenched, his eyes wild. His giant footsteps squashed pumpkins, beet greens, and brambles with no thought to Clangsy's hard work. Without a moment's hesitation, Jack hopped off the goose, reached down, and parted the clouds where they were pierced by the beanstalk. Then he leapt back on the goose and yelled, "Fly!"

Seconds later, Garwin peered down through that same hole in the clouds and shouted, "Goose, Goose. Come back. Come back." But that disloyal goose continued to fly downward not caring she was accomplice to a theft.

Garwin glanced back at Clangsy, who stood wordlessly by, eyes wide with fright. For the very first time, the words of the fortune teller made sense to her. Jack was the Measly man Garwin feared. "Garwin! No!"

If Garwin heard Clangsy, he gave no sign. Garwin grasped the beanstalk between his knees and started to slide down. His situation was precarious; a beanstalk sturdy enough for a Measly man to climb would not, could not bear the weight of a Giant. The stalk began to sway, dipping lower, lower, and lower as Clangsy watched in horror. The wind rushed through Garwin's hair and ballooned his shirt. She reached down through the hole in the clouds as though she could snatch her husband back, but he was too far away.

"Garwin," she sobbed. Her tears fell on him like rain and soaked his clothes, making him heavier and heavier. "Garwin," she cried. "I never—"

"Claaaaangsy," he yelled, the sound echoing off the mountains below and the clouds above.

Finally, the beanstalk snapped in two and Garwin was airborne. "Claaaangsy," Garwin yelled as he crashed down, carving out a giant-size hole and setting off an earthquake in both the underworld and Cloud Country above. There was the sound of thousands of trees snapping like matchsticks, the crashing of rocks as the hole caved in deeper and deeper. "Clangsssyyyy," Garwin boomed as tears poured from his eyes.

Her tears mingled with his, and together they filled the crater, becoming a sea of salt water. He gasped for air as the tears closed over his mouth, his nose. Oh, it was a dreadful sight to see this Giant unable to move as rocks continued to slide into the great hole. Clangsy kept her vigil as bubbles percolated up through the sea, but she heard from Garwin no more.

If you think the story ends with Garwin's death and Jack living happily ever after, rich with the goose that laid the golden eggs, you would be wrong. As soon as the goose flew beyond Garwin's reach, she shook Jack off her back and flew to freedom. Jack landed safely and wandered around for days trying to return home, having to circle around the newly formed sea. The king's soldiers arrested him for wanton destruction of what once had been the king's favorite hunting preserve. And Clangsy? She moved in with Bangor and they lived almost happily ever after.

FELICIA AND THE BARON

T.J. Young

Baron Eustace von Tinklebaum III was a rich and powerful man. This entitled him to certain privileges, as one might expect of a Baron. In his youth, these privileges took a trivial form, such as stepping on people's toes when they weren't looking and blaming it on others, and sneezing without covering his nose or mouth. When he got older and succeeded to the baronetcy, however, his privileges became more expansive and more eclectic. For example, he claimed the right to sit in the best box at the local opera house, the right to park his carriage wherever he chose—even in the middle of the street, and the right to appropriate the best fabrics and buttons from the local haberdasheries.

These in themselves were not remarkable, having been claimed by many previous barons, but von Tinklebaum III went even further. He claimed the privilege not only of sitting in the best box at the opera, but also the right to interrupt the performance with his own ejaculations—snorts, grunts, cries, guffaws, expressions of disgust or alarm, and other noises—no matter how inappropriate or poorly timed they might be. On one occasion, the Baron even shouted at the performers, yelling, "Fie, fie!," for no apparent reason, startling one of them so greatly the poor man fell headfirst into the orchestra pit and would have fractured his skull were he not wearing an enormous wig at the time. Because of these outbursts, the Baron was viewed by his subjects with some suspicion, and even malice.

To be sure, the Baron's opera privileges were insignificant compared to others that he enjoyed, such as the privilege of descending on the local taverns with his full entourage of courtiers, courtesans, guards, jugglers, and musicians, demanding to be provided with a full five course meal including ale and a baked desert, without any prior warning. Or the privilege of commandeering the local farmer's fields for an impromptu archery contest. Or, perhaps most spectacularly, the privilege of squeezing the buttocks of the local peasants' wives; although the Baron had learned to exercise this last privilege sparingly, having more than once had his nose painfully bloodied by the woman in question.

But it was his operatic privileges that the Baron most zealously treasured. He was, in fact, a lover of the finer things, a collector and patron of the arts, and indeed himself occasionally played the pianoforte or the flute, although he found that the latter tended to cause his guests to excuse themselves more quickly than usual and sometimes even led to howling by the palace contingent of hunting dogs.

Because of these privileges, the Baron was, on the whole, happy. His lands were prosperous, his fingernails were well-trimmed, his jesters were at least occasionally funny, and his bed did not squeak unduly. His wine cellar was nearly always full, the roof of the palace did not leak—except in the guest rooms, and the sycophants and underlings with which he surrounded himself were easily changed when he became bored with them. Since he was happy, the Baron assumed that his subjects were also happy, but on this point he was sadly mistaken. Many of his subjects were not happy at all. Not only did they resent his privileges, they also suffered significant hardships of which the Baron, being cosseted in the lap of luxury, was entirely ignorant. Unhappiest of all were those imprisoned in the infamous dungeons that existed underneath the palace. These unfortunate souls were very unhappy indeed. The Baron, however, seldom thought about them, having discovered that a visit to the dungeons involved a number of disagreeable sights and sounds, and even on one occasion resulted in one of the prisoners baring his buttocks at the Baron and shouting, "Squeeze this, you bastard," in what was apparently intended as a parody of the Baron's privilege relating thereto. The man had, of course, been flogged, but the taint remained.

Recently, however, the Baron had become aware of an inexplicable decline in his happiness; he was plagued by a nagging feeling of dissatisfaction that he couldn't quite place. This decline began when one of his guards discovered a young woman hiding in an empty wine cask who, when the cask was opened, brandished a large knife and started repeatedly shouting, "Death to the tyrant!" The guard naturally concluded she was an assassin, so he took the knife away and brought her before the Baron, where he assumed she would be banished to the dungeons. The Baron, at the time, was sitting in his favorite chair eating a large bunch of particularly succulent grapes. Being thus absorbed, and in any case slightly bored that day, he failed to listen to or fully appreciate the guard's rendition of the facts regarding her discovery. As a result, he mistakenly assumed the young woman was just a harmless courtesan who had got drunk and fallen asleep in the cask by mistake. It was not uncommon after some of the Baron's more risqué parties for one or more of the guests to fall asleep in unusual and often embarrassing locations, such as the rooftop chimneys, the flowerpots in the garden, or even the Baron's own bed. Thus, he simply waved the woman away, instructing the guard to take her back to her room.

He was about to resume eating his grapes when the woman suddenly rushed toward him, brandishing yet another knife she had apparently concealed in her stocking and which the rather inept guard had failed to discover. The Baron, not noticing the knife, which was quite small and had an ornamental handle made of walrus ivory, thought she intended to embrace him. He considered this odd given the circumstances, but, being a magnanimous man, he nevertheless opened his ams wide to receive her. This gesture naturally startled the woman, since she did not expect to be welcomed, causing her to pause momentarily. Then, when she sprang forward, she slipped on a stray grape that had found its way onto the floor and instead of stabbing the Baron in the chest as she had envisioned, she fell awkwardly and rather suggestively into his lap. The knife thus succeeded only in impaling a pillow the Baron habitually kept there to conceal the paunch he had developed in recent years.

The Baron, impressed with her apparently amorous intentions, lifted her from his lap and gazed smilingly into her eyes with much more interest than he typically exhibited. It was this moment of accidental intimacy that marked the beginning of the Baron's peculiar sense of dissatisfaction. He saw something in her eyes he did not expect—not exactly a spark, but more of a burning coal, lurking in the depths of her surprisingly large and attractive brown eyes. This coal—or perhaps it was merely the shadow of a coal—somehow lodged in his consciousness and settled there, slowly working its way further and further into the somewhat fatty tissue of the Baron's heart. Of course, the clear view the Baron had of the young woman's nearly bare, exceptionally voluptuous, chest may also have contributed to the warm feeling which he experienced during their encounter.

In fact, the young woman—whose name was Felicia Larue—hated the Baron, and the guard had correctly divined that her intention was indeed to assassinate him. She and her family were tavern owners who belonged to a dissident political faction that regarded the Baron as a parasite. The Baron had imprisoned her father years earlier because, in a bold gesture of political defiance, the father had served the Baron, during one of his unwelcome and unscheduled visits to the family tavern, a pie in the shape of a hand with its middle finger extended. The Baron, either oblivious to the symbolism or too hungry to care, had eaten the pie and found it delicious but later that evening he had become quite ill, a circumstance for which he blamed the father, even though it was far more likely that the Baron's illness resulted from the large quantity of ale he drank that night.

Whatever the cause, the Baron accused the father of attempting to poison him and the man, consistent with his political beliefs, had replied that he wished he *had* poisoned him—whereupon the Baron ordered his arrest and the man was dragged away to the dungeons while his wife and daughter hid behind the bar and cried silently into their skirts. Unbeknownst to Felicia, this same man, her father, was the prisoner who had so rudely exposed his buttocks to the Baron from his prison cell during one of the Baron's rare visits to the dungeons. The man apparently had a gift—or at least a compulsion—for creative, if ultimately empty, political gestures.

Felicia, being a dutiful daughter, had vowed revenge on the Baron and had plotted her knife attack for several months. Unfortunately, as we have already seen, the attack went awry. This was not due to any fault of her own but resulted from the fact that the palace guard whom she had inveigled into giving her information about the Baron had been grossly in error regarding the nature of the wine cask in which she had hidden. He had told her the cask would be delivered directly to the Baron's bedchamber where, according to the guard, the Baron planned to use it as a planter for some ferns of which he was fond. Relying on this information, she had quickly dispatched the guard by cracking him over the head with a wine bottle. She then crawled into the cask, assuming she would soon be delivered to the Baron.

What she had neglected to consider, however, was that the guard's information was inherently suspect, since at the time he had told her about the cask he was lying on top of her in a corner of the storeroom, eagerly removing her underclothes, with what up until then had been her slyly calculated cooperation and encouragement. She had, perhaps, underestimated the strength of her allure, for at the moment in question the man was so desperate, with his fingers fumbling at the buttons of her corset, he likely would have told her just about anything. In truth, he had no idea where the cask was headed and his story about the ferns was entirely invented.

All was not lost, however, as far as Felicia's plans were concerned, because the Baron never discovered the ivory-handled knife embedded in his lap pillow. Upon leaving the Baron after their encounter over the grapes, she had been taken to a luxurious suite in a wing of the palace and left there more or less to her own devices. The suite—filled as it was with expensive fabrics, pillows, lotions, and many other amenities—was superficially pleasing, but it also increased her sense of outrage and injustice, as it stood in such stark contrast to the hardship she knew many of the Baron's subjects experienced. Especially those locked in the dungeons just below her. Thus, while she enjoyed the suite's many luxuries, it did not soften her resolve. She remained steadfast in her purpose; plotting and scheming with all the cleverness she had inherited from her father, but with greater subtlety.

The Baron, meanwhile, resumed the rounds of eating and drinking, archery and opera, piano and flute, with which he filled his days. Once or twice he caught a glimpse of Felicia amongst his entourage, but he had no idea that she harbored murderous intentions towards him. He assumed she was just another courtesan, although one as to which he harbored a special feeling he could never quite identify. Every time he saw her, he felt that peculiar, nagging sense of dissatisfaction in his heart, and he seemed to see before him once again the startled, wide-eyed look she had on her face when she had fallen into his lap. It was an image he could not shake—similar, at least in his own mind, to the way in which he could not shake the mint sauce off his fingers after eating a roast leg of lamb.

It was with some surprise then, as well as trepidation, that the Baron found himself asking Felicia to dance with him at the annual Teetotaler's Ball, an event which, despite its name, involved the consumption of large amounts of alcoholic beverages, often mixed together in surprising and not altogether palatable combinations. The Baron gazed at her fondly as they twirled around the dance floor, his heart beating more rapidly than usual, a sense of warm satisfaction suffusing his body, and a haze of inebriation obscuring his vision. Because of this haze, and his general air of comfort and well-being, he failed to notice that Felicia was craftily edging him closer and closer to the large windows that ran the length of the ballroom on one side. These windows, which gave onto a view of the gardens, were open to the fragrant night air, and since the ballroom was on the third floor, they were about thirty feet above the rock-hard gravel of the walkway below.

Within minutes, Felicia maneuvered the Baron up to one of these windows, and with a sudden, violent thrust, pushed him over the sill. Startled, the Baron flew backwards out the window and, with hardly even a squeak, disappeared. So quick and so unexpected was this action, that none of the other guests even noticed it. The string orchestra at the far end of the ballroom played on, and the dancers continued to swirl about the room in waves of taffeta, silk, and heavy perfume. His disappearance was unremarkable because, frankly, he often disappeared from his balls, usually either to pass out in the hall or to throw up in the privy chamber. Felicia, after glancing around and observing the lack of reaction on the part of the guests, with a sly smile on her face, dared to take a peek over the windowsill—she longed to see the Baron's broken body lying on the path and was prepared to exult in his demise. To her astonishment, however, this is not what she saw.

Instead of lying broken on the path below, the Baron was sitting comfortably in the foliage of a cypress tree that happened to be growing just outside the window. Serendipitously, this tree had been transplanted by the Baron to that location only that very day. He had been strolling in the gardens that morning and observed what he thought was some unsightly graffiti scratched into the wall of the palace just below the window in question. To hide this, he had instructed his gardeners to transplant the cypress tree in front of it. In fact, the markings he had observed were not graffiti —they were a commemorative inscription that had been carved there years earlier by the Baron's grandfather, von Tinklebaum I, on the occasion of his having eaten a record number of mince pies. *Many and meaty were these minces,* it read, *which have this day met their match,* followed by the date and the grandfather's name. The Baron had completely forgotten about this feat and his gardeners, perhaps wisely, refrained from pointing it out.

In any case, the Baron's punctiliousness worked to his advantage, and indeed, likely saved his life. As he sat there in the arms of the cypress, he happened to look up and see Felicia looking down at him. In his alcoholic stupor, he interpreted her expression as one of concern and compassion. He could not, for the life of him, figure out how he had ended up in the tree, but he assumed it was due to his own clumsiness and inebriation. He thus looked up at Felicia with a hopeful and somewhat rueful expression—he hoped fervently that she would forgive him his clumsiness and still accept him as her dance partner. He had found that being with her eased the dissatisfaction in his heart, and returned to him that sense of contentment he had been used to before they met over the grapes. He even called up to her, in an effort to make a joke of the situation, "So sorry, my dear, but this tree seems to have cut in."

Felicia, for her part, was more annoyed than amused; her look as she gazed down at him from the window was one of irritated incredulity, and she was actually cursing softly to herself, wondering where the damn tree had come from. The Baron, however, was oblivious of this. He was comfortable in the tree, and considered simply going to sleep in it, but then thought that not only would doing so probably give him a backache, he would also miss further dancing with Felicia. Thus, he eventually climbed down and found his way back to the ballroom. He looked everywhere for Felicia, but she had disappeared.

In the wake of this incident, the Baron recognized, with what was, for him, a remarkable degree of self-knowledge, that his feelings for Felicia amounted to love. He determined to woo her passionately, with all that his money could buy. He bombarded her with gifts—flowers, chocolates, cakes, dresses, liquors, and jewelry. He issued her a veritable snowstorm of invitations—to dinners, to the opera, to carriage rides, to his flute and piano recitals, to archery and riding contests. He even invited her to attend with him a public flogging, which she, of course, politely declined.

Felicia was not insensitive to these blandishments—many of them, such as the flute recitals, were excruciatingly painful, but others, such as the chocolates and the flowers, were not unpleasant, and some, like riding, she even enjoyed. She found the Baron's courtship ironically amusing, if not actually insane, and she often found herself laughing uproariously while alone in her bedchamber over his latest inept attempt to charm her. His poetry, in particular, she could hardly read without breaking into helpless giggles. But while laughing at the Baron was almost as good a form of revenge as doing him harm, it was not enough. When she thought of her father, unjustly imprisoned, languishing half naked in the dungeon below, her blood still boiled and she fell again to plotting the Baron's death. She considered using the Baron's ludicrous regard for her as a means of tricking him into releasing her father, but she realized she wanted more than just his release—she wanted the Baron to suffer; she wanted revenge.

She tried on several occasions to dispatch the Baron, but each time some freak chance of nature intervened to save him. At an archery contest, for example, she managed to take a shot at him, but just as she loosed the arrow, he bent over to wipe from his hose a stray blob of half-eaten pate, so the arrow whizzed over his head and struck a grouse instead, which everyone assumed was the intended target. The Baron even praised her aim, and awarded her a silver-plated bow as a prize. On another occasion, while riding, she contrived to steer the Baron's horse toward a steep river embankment, where she hoped the horse would jump into the water and, with luck, the Baron would be swept away and drown. But while the horse did indeed jump off the embankment, the Baron did not go with it—he had drunk too much champagne that morning and had difficulty finding his stirrups; as a result, he accidentally slipped off the horse and fell harmlessly to the ground before the horse even reached the embankment. Thus, the only result of her effort was that the horse got soaked and subsequently came down with the horse equivalent of a bad cold.

These failures naturally irritated Felicia, but since the Baron, blind with love or lust, or perhaps just with alcohol, never suspected her, he continued his courtship as ardently as ever. He regarded his escape from these accidents as, if anything, a sign of divine favor, as another kind of privilege—the privilege of being lucky in a dangerous world. He even viewed Felicia as a form of protection—as if she insulated him from harm. Indeed, Felicia herself, as her failures mounted, begin to have this same view—that her efforts, far from dispatching the Baron, were somehow saving him instead. As perverse as it might seem, she could see no other explanation. Night after night, when not laughing at the Baron's latest poem, she stewed over this conundrum. Eventually, she made a fateful decision. She resolved to make one last, sure-fire effort to kill the Baron, which she fervently hoped would succeed; but if it did not, if she failed again, she would instead take a different course. She would try to make him happy, make every effort to please him—even marry him if he asked—and in that way, hopefully, she might actually succeed in getting rid of him.

Thus it was that their brief affair—if one could call it that—came to a head. The Baron invited Felicia to the opera and she accepted. She had, by this time, retrieved the ivory handled knife that had become lost in the Baron's lap pillow those weeks ago, and she concealed it in her voluminous skirts. Her plan was simple—at a critical moment during the performance, when the music was at a crescendo, she would stab the Baron and then make her escape before his body could be discovered. Admittedly, the plan was somewhat vague in its details, especially regarding the exact method of her escape, but she was unconcerned—she trusted in her ingenuity, the high level of inebriation among the opera guests, the laxity of the Baron's guards, and the fact that, when necessary, she could sprint like the wind.

As they approached the opera house, Felicia trembled with

anticipation. She wore one of her most revealing dresses, correctly concluding that her décolletage would distract the Baron from his peril. When they took their seats in the Baron's box, she contrived to sit as close to him as possible, and fluffed out her skirts so that they completely covered her seat and partially overlayed the Baron's lap. The Baron, charmed and amused by what he took to be her flirtation, smiled at her and tried to pinch her thigh. He was excited by her proximity, and his heart fairly bubbled with joy to think that she looked upon him with as much affection as he looked upon her.

One thing did, however, trouble him. That morning he had had had a dream in which he was walking with her through a garden of flowers while birds flew overhead. That was pleasant enough, but then the sky darkened and an apple fell from a tree. When they both bent to pick it up, they bonked heads, and she had laughed maniacally while the Baron fell backward in a swoon. Unsure how to interpret this dream, which left him with a slight headache, he had puzzled over it for an hour or so while lying in bed. Did it signify a shared destiny, he wondered, or something else? The Baron could not decide. Eventually he concluded the problem was beyond his ken, so he simply forgot about it and turned his attention to breakfast. The episode, however, left him feeling slightly giddy, a feeling which persisted while he was at the opera.

It was, perhaps, this lingering feeling of giddiness, or perhaps it was the excitement induced by the nearness and splendor of Felicia's décolletage, that led the Baron to, at the climax of the opera, leap upward and shout, "Fie, fie," at the performers, as it was, at least in his own mind, his privilege to do. Coincidentally, it was at this same moment that Felicia decided to stab the Baron with the ivory handled knife. The result was that the knife, instead of penetrating the Baron's vital organs, struck him in the buttocks instead, where the Baron had, before leaving for the opera, tucked a flask of spirits which he often took to the opera in case any emergency requiring such spirits should arise. The knife pierced the flask but did not reach the Baron's skin. Felicia, startled by the Baron's sudden movement, tried to withdraw the knife so as to strike again, but it became wedged in the silver of the flask and stuck there. When the Baron reseated himself, the knife disappeared in the cushions of the seat and Felicia could not reach it.

Stunned that her plan had apparently failed yet again, Felicia could barely conceal her consternation. The Baron, meanwhile, suddenly noticed that his breeches were soaking wet. Assuming that he had, in his excitement, inadvertently wet himself, the Baron hurriedly excused himself and, in a state of intense embarrassment, headed for the men's lounge. Felicia, seeing in his departure an opportunity to snatch victory from the jaws of defeat, excused herself also and raced after him. As the Baron passed through the lobby en route to the lounge, the knife's ivory handle was plainly visible protruding from his rear. This led the various footmen and others in the lobby to smirk behind their hands as the Baron passed, but the Baron assumed this was due to his incontinence rather than any other cause. He resolved to punish them later and rushed on, Felicia only a few steps behind.

They both arrived more or less simultaneously in the privacy of the lounge. When the door shut behind them, they were alone; no one else was there. The Baron, hearing the rustle of her skirts, turned toward her. Her face was flushed, her eyes bright, her hair disheveled. The Baron, seeing her thus, felt an onrush of love so profound he could not contain himself. Despite his embarrassment, he wrapped her in his arms and kissed her passionately. Felicia, surprised and slightly disgusted, nevertheless feigned returning his kiss, while with her free hand she sought to retrieve the knife, and this time she succeeded. She pulled it free and, whispering, "Take this, tyrant," in the Baron's ear, she plunged it with all her strength into the back of his neck.

Unfortunately for her, the Baron wore an excessive amount of jewelry, including an ornate clasp at the back of his cravat. The blade struck this clasp and, weakened by its various adventures, instead of penetrating his neck, it broke and fell harmlessly to the ground. The Baron, mishearing what she had whispered, assumed she had declared her love for him and kissed her again and again. Felicia, seeing out of the corner of her eye the knife blade lying unbloodied on the floor, sighed, swore briefly under her breath, then, remembering her resolve, she forced herself to kiss him back.

They were married two months later in a lavish ceremony at the palace. The Baron thought it strange when, as he carried her upstairs to the bridal chamber, she smiled and said "this had better work," but he was too excited and eager to give it any thought. Amazingly, however, it actually did work, for no sooner did he jump into bed with Felicia and seek to consummate his marriage, then the enormous quantity of frosting he had eaten from the wedding cake plugged his already strained heart. His eyes went wide, he emitted a loud groan and, for some obscure reason, the word "oops," then fell stone dead on the floor. Felicia, hardly believing her eyes, at first broke into peals of laughter at this result, then realized such behavior was more than slightly suspicious, so she quickly composed herself, called for help and shed copious, if phony, tears.

Her performance must have been convincing, because the people readily accepted her as their new Baroness and hardly mourned the dead Baron at all. They even applauded her first act, which was to set all the prisoners held in the dungeons, including her father, free. Reunited with him, she ruled wisely for many years and did what she could to ease the hardships of her subjects. She renounced all of the excessive privileges the prior Baron had so rudely exercised, gave away much of his wealth, and she never once shouted "fie" at the opera. She did, however, occasionally visit the Baron's grave, and leave there a little piece of their wedding cake—which she carefully preserved—in memory of his demise.

MRS. SPITTLEBERG SERVES THE TWO SISTERS TEA

Jenn Hopkins

It had been the fifth day of flashfloods and firestorms, and the people of the village of West Buribarren were getting rather tired of it. Many had complaints, but few had the courage to say anything.

Alice Willis, having drawn the short straw, approached the mayor, "You know I can't even get my children across the bridge to school. The river has drowned out the riverside roads. This ridiculous feud has gotten out of hand. Can you not speak to them?"

"Them" were the Sisters North and South. North was the Sister of Water and South was the Sister of Fire and on most occasions they were rather congenial, if a bit opinionated.

Alice was from the North district, the one ruled by Water. She was the only one cued up to speak with the mayor on their behalf (they being such busy professionals that they were of the opinion that only one of their number need petition the powers-that-be),

171

but there was a long line of smoky and ash-covered complainants from the South district, the district ruled by Fire. They were getting rather tired of the rampant flames flaring up all over their backyards, houses, business places and parks. Sal Torino had lost an entire season's worth of ice cream from his truck, tires melted to the cobblestones and the sagging vehicle whirring, a droning and wobbly version of "Pop Goes the Weasel" that made children run away crying, and many adults worry that his truck had been possessed.

The disasters did not confine themselves to their districts. The East District, the district of Wind, was finding itself overwhelmed with the amount of flames that they needed to blow out. But Wind was only a cousin to the two sisters therefore not powerful enough (certainly not loud enough) to stop them. Earth, being a bit of a glutton, was completely apathetic toward those of his constituents abiding in the West District who were bothered by such things. They were forced to move on to the upper mountains of Walladria, a place occupied by ice spirits who were mostly benevolent toward humans (though they tended to hate wolves more—as long as they bothered the wolves and not the spirits themselves).

The mayor was beside himself. In all his ten years of office the Elementals had had little tiffs between one another, but never such an all out feverish war.

Some of the townspeople had started taking up arms—well, hoes and pitchforks—against each other hoping that their show of solidarity with their Elemental would spare them further damage to their homes, families and persons. The mayor fretted at the sight of them. He knew this would greatly damage his re-electability. His assistant then reminded him that he should also care for his constituents' welfare.

"I guess," he told her. "If you're into that sort of thing. So we should . . ."

"Do something to help them," she explained, wondering if her daily activity of pointing out the obvious would some day merit her a raise.

"Yes, yes, of course."

He smiled confidently, but she could see the blankness in his eyes, so she put in, "We should find a consultant who knows how to work with the Elementals?"

"Yes, of course!" he elated, then stood staring at her.

She sighed, fetched the Book of Consultants and plopped it on his desk.

"Oh, yes! That!" he said in awed wonder at such an amazing discovery, then flipped through it.

He first went to the Servator of the Temples, an older, languid man who often seemed asleep even as he walked. He dressed in the old fashioned, white robes as his office dictated, but never seemed to change out of them, as he felt his job to be an all encompassing ordeal. Few of his attendants could ever capture his attention—he was too busy saving their souls.

"Servator," said the mayor, "what would you do?"

The Servator put a finger to his lip and considered. It was then that Mrs. Spittleberg bounced in joyfully, a hat of flowers on her head and many aprons on her person.

"Good day, sir Mayor, I see that the fairies are favoring your belly." She pat said belly.

The mayor sighed, for Mrs. Spittleberg was a silly woman who spoke in riddles and served teacakes to fairies from her back porch.

"Please, Mrs. Spittleberg," wailed the mayor, "we are discussing serious matters; we are trying to decide how to end the feud of the Two Sisters."

"Oh! I should think that that would be quite simple," she sang.

"Yes, yes, you would think that," said the Servator, waving her aside. "From our point of view it is very complex indeed! We have done all of the proper sacrifices and said all the proper incantations, therefore there must be a ceremony that has not been properly abided. I shall have to consult the mystics."

"Are you certain?" asked Mrs. Spittleberg innocently. "Should you not try to join hands and pray with them?"

The Servator showed her his droll disdain at such a ludicrous question. "How little you know of the mystical," he stated. "In all the texts in all the land, never has such a ridiculous notion ever been even somewhat hinted at. No, the Templionian Patriarchy is infinitely wise. We shall do as they advise and get the proper ritual started."

"Oh, do hurry!" said the mayor. "Things have quite gotten out of hand."

And the mystics were consulted and they said that everyone should go with drums to the houses of the Sisters (one in the Southern District, the other in the Northern) and sing, chant and drum as loudly as possible.

Unsurprisingly, this only seemed to greatly irritate the Sisters more and the floods and firestorms increased in volume.

Greatly panicked, the mayor went to the leader of the Intellectuals and asked what would be the philosophical solution. Again Mrs. Spittleberg barged in singing, "Oh, what great and complex thoughts they have, but really I must emphasize that it is all very simple."

She was shushed by Falcon, the lead Intellectual. "There is nothing that reason cannot solve," they told the Mayor. "For as wild as we know them to be, we also know that they always have a plan and anything with a plan must have reason. Reason shall rule."

"Hmmm," hummed Mrs. Spittleberg, "but does reason always rule?"

Falcon just shook their head at her, thoroughly disappointed, and left for their commune to devise a clever treatise that no Elemental could refute.

But as sound as their argument was, as iron clad their logic, when they approached the Sisters with the very astute observation of, "now, you're both just being irrational," the hospital found that they needed to treat the Intellectuals with both second-degree burns and third-degree waterlogging.

The mayor rushed to Sergeant at Arms, Harry Harrisbrattle-Bottom.

"I know that it would be a bad idea to shoot at them, but perhaps the threat of firearms would discourage them?" the mayor pondered. "Or drive them into their homes where they could cool down and think things through?"

Harry grit his teeth, a steely glint in his eye.

"This has gone beyond quiet contemplation, sir!" he yelled as he often did. "These are unruly women who lack in discipline. What they really need is a good pistol whipping. No one in this town has ever called them out for their terrible manners!" He waved his finger like a teacher's ruler threatening his students. "They believe that they can do whatever they like Willy Nilly, act out as they please . . ." But just as his voice reached a glorious uproar, a giggle erupted from a corner. And there was Mrs. Spittleberg giggling into her hand, holding back roils of laughter.

The Mayor's shoulders clinched. His face turned redder than his official strawberry sash (the town's representational fruit).

"Ignore her!" he told Harrisbrattle-Bottom. "She has been tending to do this, showing up at the least convenient of moments acting all a fool. With nothing useful to add!" He stated that last sentence furrowing his brows at her giggles.

"Oh, no," Harrisbrattle-Bottom's voice was provocative, "by all means, such a helpful and obviously wise woman must have a fountain full of information. Please, douse us with your canyon river of knowledge."

She blinked at both of them with bright and puzzled blinks. "Truly?" she asked. "Well, I am sincerely blessed by Master Sergeant at Arms, I have never heard those terms put quite so . . . creatively," her head buzzed happily as she said it. "But I do worry that you do not understand what it is exactly that you are saying, for you see, the Sisters do not need discipline. They are not acting wild. They are Wildness incarnate. I fear that your guns and your snares and your bombs and sharp objects will do little to impress them. I would advise you to instead harness that incredible head for strategy and find a way to keep the people out of harm from their little tete-a-tete."

She then beamed a smile at him thinking him most complimented by her loving praise, so was most confused when he turned a gritting frown at her.

"You think me a coward, don't you?" he asked.

"Why no, sir," she answered quite plainly. "You are the least cowardly of all the men in all the village—at least the Eastern Sector of it."

"Oh, of course, this is what you think! Not hiding your scorn behind all those honeyed words?"

She shook her head. "No, sir, not at all!"

"And you!" he shouted at the Mayor. "You let this— this shrew, speak to me this way?"

"Wh-what?" the Mayor babbled. "No, no, of course not."

"You think me a coward! Well, I shall show you all!" And with that Harrisbrattle-Bottom marched back to his barracks, requisitioned all the guns he could carry, and made haste for the Sisters.

"If they should act as the enemy," he said to himself, "then, by God, we shall treat them so!"

He rushed the Sister of the South, firing around her. "These are warning shots, Sister! The next will be fatal! You shall back down from all of this nonsense! Now!"

South swirled round and shot a glare of scorn. Her fiery red hair flared brighter from its wild and twirling updo. She brushed at her glamorous, ruffled, red, satin gown and furrowed a glinting brow.

"You dare fire rounds at me!" she shouted.

"This is your final warning!" He ratcheted his gun.

"This fight is none of your concern!"

"I have been put in charge here! You will do as I say!"

"Leave now!" Smoke drifted from her mouth.

But he stood before her, unmoved. Sister South shot a hand forward as he shot his gun. His fired bullet was melted long before it reached its target—but her fire did reach him.

His screams were heard all across the ten counties. Sister

North rushed forward.

"Sister, no!" she yelled. "We have sworn not to kill them—at least, not too terribly much."

"He dared fire his gun at me!" yelled Sister South.

"He did what!" Sister North grit icy teeth at him. Her sea foam hair writhed in hurricanic waves. All of the icicles adorning her onesie jumpsuit shivered stormily. She raised up her arms and a ten-foot tall wave rose up, dousing Harrisbrattle-Bottom into a fold of water that swept him all the way out to a lake seven counties away.

"They have sent their arms against us?" steamed Sister North. "Violence against us? US!! Providers of warmth and water for their crops and cattle! They think they can get away with this? Do you hear us, Mayor! We shall not stand for this ingratitude!"

"I beg your pardon," said Sister South. "He was firing at me! I'm the one who should be teaching them a lesson!"

"He fires at you, he fires at both of us! Why can you not think of anyone but yourself!"

"I don't need you to fight my battles! I am just as powerful as you are! If not more so!"

"I'll show you power, my selfish sister!"

And the torment grew worse, until the town was engulfed with clashes of waters and flames.

"Oh!" wailed the Mayor. This was worse than the simple fighting. "Now, they're angry at us! Oh, no, oh, no! Whatever shall we do?"

And he ran, inviting all the town to follow and evacuate out of the disaster areas.

The mayor ran up the mountain and into his stone bunker

with the rest of the town. All huddled there wringing their hands, Alice Willis standing off in a corner surrounded by whinging children, her arms folded as she murmured, "Why'd I even bother?"

"What should we do?" the mayor burst out. "Soon we shall have no more town!"

"Echem!" Mrs. Spittleberg cleared her throat. "Perhaps I could..."

The mayor moaned petulantly. "Fine! Fine!" he said and waved at her to get on to it.

Joyfully, Mrs. Spittleberg splashed her way home and put out several muffins, her most sacred and wondrous biscuits, and the loveliest of lovely packets of tea, onto the center table in the quaint living room of her house which had oddly been untouched by fire or flood. She rang up both Sisters and invited them to her place.

"First and foremost," she said on the telephone, "I cannot emphasize more that I am not associated with any of the humans who have previously visited. But I shall, indeed, emphatically apologize for their ridiculous behavior. Lilac Lillyfoot, my hedge pixie, should be sending over some beautiful flowers as we speak as a show of my endearing love and honor to you both."

Both sisters agreed that the bouquets were most splendid—more so than any assemblage of flowers they'd ever seen and, thus, they agreed to the meet.

When the Sisters arrived, both growling at one another, Mrs. Spittleberg would not allow them entry.

"I must apologize," she told them, "but I cannot have fire or water damage to my little house. It is all I have in the world. I shall make you the loveliest tea and give you the grandest muffins and biscuits, but you must both agree to be civil while you are here.

I ask humbly and prostrate myself before you and your beautiful mercy."

The Sisters both considered, still feeling very stung by their last encounter with a human, but seeing how small and pathetic Mrs. Spittleberg had made herself, finally, they nodded, and she let them enter. Mrs. Spittleberg brewed them tea, set out all of the dainty items and gossiped with them. She told them how very silly and petty all these humans were with their silly, petty obsessions, and petty, silly gestures, all working so very hard to seem so very important.

"As if the ones they were trying to make themselves look important for were even considered," she quipped.

She tittled all about the romantic intrigues of the Coyote twins and tattled all about the strange machinations of the House Balou. She dished about Mrs. Orchid and her obsession with Mrs. Gulaag's hat collection. She whispered all about Master Grummand and his loud brags of how his carriage was the fanciest and the most expensive. Then she told them about her sweet grandmother and of her passing this many year ago. And then spoke of her sister and her tragic and untimely death.

"We fought a lot and about everything, but deep down I knew that we loved each other. Late at night, she would sneak from her room and whisper all of her secrets and I would whisper mine and if our parents caught us, we would get in terrible trouble.

"But the day before she tripped and fell from that cliff, I had told her how much I despised her and now I would do anything— anything under all the Heavens or all the Earths—to see her just once more to tell her I loved her. Just one more intrigue, one more ill advised adventure . . . one more shared trouble."

She fluttered her fingers against her chest and looked up to the Great Beyond in the hope of that one final glimpse that never came.

Sister Water fluttered her lashes at Sister Fire. One shed a tear and the other a drop of magma. They both embraced one another with a warm sizzle and gushed about how sorry the one was to the other.

And the fires were quenched by the floods and the floods dried by the fires and the town became quiet once again.

The mayor heartily thanked Mrs. Spittleberg. "We must recommend you for the Medal of Great Epicness and shall consult you for all future catastrophes," he extolled.

"Now, now," said Mrs. Spittleberg, "let us let it pass, for it was not me who did the saving, it was the tea."

SKY CRICKET; OR, HOW MOON BEAR AND CLOUDED LEOPARD BECAME THEMSELVES

Michael Heyman

In the days when the moon burned brighter and the clouds hung closer, a cricket pitch stretched itself across the top of the world near the village of Chail. This was no ordinary pitch, however, but the only patch of earth close enough to the moon and clouds for Sky Cricket. Around the windswept sward, at the top of the world, clung the world's last trees and caves, and from the last trees and caves watched the eyes that knew the villagers never once played properly: they played Wrong Cricket.

Every evening in August, the Astronomer of Chail checked the stars to see if it was the Right Time for Wrong Cricket. If three shooting stars intersected with Saptarshi, or the Seven Sages, the Astronomer would ring a bell ten times to signal the whole village. The villagers welcomed the sound of the bell, but none more than Akshay, the Juggler's son. Akshay knew that a game of cricket meant much more than the game; it was an adventure to the top of the world with his family, to ride the world's last winds like one of the brittle leaves that blow up and up, never to come back to earth. But more than anything else, a game of cricket meant that his father, who was the greatest Juggler in all the Himalayas, would juggle.

In the mornings after the ten bell toll, Akshay was always the first out of the house. Soon he, his father, mother, and grandmother, and the other villagers of Chail would climb the stairs, stone by stone, that wound up and around the hill, until they could hear the waves of wind washing past the highest leaves, out beyond the world. They bore bats and balls, picnic baskets, blankets, and pillows. Some played Wrong Cricket while the others lounged on pillows and drank cold drinks, and then the players drank cold drinks and lounged on pillows while the others played Wrong Cricket. Akshay's family sat a little away from the rest of the villagers.

During the game's slow patches, Akshay's father would juggle to entertain the younger children. He might begin with a few cricket balls, first three, then seven, then ten, but soon he would add snails, stones, stoats, and anything else he found lying or hanging or slinking about. He would juggle standing on one foot. Then he would juggle *only* with his feet. Akshay's father was, indeed, the greatest Juggler in all the Himalayas, but only the children watched his performances.

All the while, unbeknownst to Akshay, his family, and the villagers, silent eyes watched from the world's last trees and caves.

When the players tired of lounging and the loungers tired of playing, they packed up their bats and balls, picnic baskets, blankets, and pillows, and wound their way stone by stone back down the hill to their homes, where they tucked into pots of steaming stew and their beds. Before falling asleep, Akshay asked his grandmother why they always left the cricket pitch at night.

"That is when the beasts play Sky Cricket—but it's not for us to see."

"Why not?"

But his grandmother would say no more.

High above, in the darkness, the cricket pitch stood silent. Nothing stirred but the tattered, world-weary winds, and the eyes that still stared from the world's last trees and caves. And then, moonlight crackled across the smooth pitch. The game had begun.

Leopard leapt from her tree soundlessly and stalked the boundary made of clay and stardust. When Bear emerged claw by tooth from his cave, they faced each other, growling. Leopard bowled a jagged boulder straight towards Bear. With a tree-trunk bat, Bear connected in a burst of splinters, sending the rock skidding across the sky as he grunted his way between the creases of bearded moss. After such a hit, the rock did not fall back to earth, as clouds fielded the hit. The wind was umpire. When Leopard was up, she swung an elephant thighbone, connecting with a shattering crack. Sometimes the boulder would bounce by their bats and smash into the wickets made from teetering wedges of frozen waterfall, showering the field in ice shards. Such was Sky Cricket.

When the growling, grunting, shard splintering, and rock cracking drifted back down the hill to the village and through Akshay's window, he sat up. It *had* to be Sky Cricket. He thought for a moment about his grandmother's warning and her silence as he put on his shoes. He tiptoed past her as she snored and then past his parents' door, out into the moonlight. He climbed the stairs, stone by stone, that wound up and around the hill, but the waves of wind washing past the highest leaves were drowned out by the strange commotion.

When he emerged onto the field, panting, Bear and Leopard turned their lamplight eyes on him. All three froze. Leopard's ears flattened and Bear bristled—and something changed. Later, when the villagers tried to note the exact moment and symptom, they talked about how the soup turned slightly salt, or the salt turned to stone, or the wind seemed to have had better things to do than finger under their doors. Akshay thought he saw the clouds and moon and stars shake loose.

When Leopard looked back to Bear, she bowled so hard that the boulder sent chunks of earth flying down the mountainside. Bear's thundering hit sent the boulder careening into the clouds but with such force that they could no longer field; they began, one by one, to be knocked to earth. With each successive hit, clouds fell like soggy cotton balls, splatting on trees and fields, and soon enough, Akshay could see them battering the houses down below in the village. And then he saw branches fall on his house, and a rain of icicles, earth, and stones, all coming from this furious match of Sky Cricket.

Arms over his head, he bounded down the stairs that wound down and around the hill, until he got back to the village where everyone was running this way and that, dodging missiles from the skies, unsure of what to do or where to go.

"Follow me!" Akshay shouted. "The cricket pitch!"

Even though he was just the Juggler's son, they followed him. While it was difficult to climb the stairs that wound up and around the hill through pelting icicles, earth, and stones, they all made it to the top, wiping clods of cloud from their wet skin. There, they could all see Leopard and Bear playing Sky Cricket so fiercely that the clouds fell, that ice cracked, that earth rained, that bone broke. If this were allowed to continue, surely their village, even the mountain itself, might be washed away and all the clouds stricken from the sky.

Bahadur the Wrestler stepped forward, saying, "I shall stop this game. Once these beasts are in my grip, they will cease and the world will be right." He squatted into his wrestling stance and circled the players, watching for an opportunity. Just after a cracking hit from Leopard's bone bat, Bahadur pounced. But he was not able to get a solid grasp—he only caught hold of Leopard's tail and Bear's left ear. With a violent shake and the most ferocious ear wag ever witnessed, Leopard and Bear sent Bahadur flying through the air and tumbling stone by stone back down the hill to his home.

Bisnu the Apple-Seller stepped to the front of the shivering crowd, saying, "I shall stop this game. Once these beasts are pelted with my apples, they will cease and the world will be right." He wheeled his apple cart near the pitch and began hurling apples quickfire. Red and green, freckled and wormed, shimmering and flecked, the apples filled the air, but rather than stopping the game, Leopard and Bear snatched the apples in flight, bowled them and hit them, sending not only clouds but also a torrent of red and mushed, freckled and smashed applesauce over the villagers.

Things were worse than ever, so Tapak the Priest shuffled

forward, saying, "I shall stop this game. Once I appeal to the heavens and our suffering is made clear, these beasts will cease and the world will be right." He began to make offerings of fragrant flowers and milk on his small altar, but he had trouble lighting incense under the clog of clouds.

As Tapak struck his damp matches over and over, Akshay could no longer contain himself. He shouted into the storm, "My father will stop this game."

This got his father's attention.

Akshay then stepped forward and faced the crowd.

"My father will juggle the ball—the stone—so high that Leopard and Bear will no longer be able to play, and the world will be right."

The villagers could only stare. Then they could only scoff, grumbling that a Juggler could never hope to right the world. But as the Priest poked at his soggy incense, and as the Wrestler and the Apple-Seller had both been defeated, they didn't know what else to do.

Akshay's father ignored their comments, and though he was the greatest Juggler in all the Himalayas, he wasn't sure his skills could save them. He looked from face to face, his fingers grasped the air. Akshay looked up at him.

Fixing his eye to the stone ball, Akshay's father stepped lightly onto the pitch. Leopard and Bear ignored the Juggler. Just as Bear bowled the stone in a vicious arc, Akshay's father sprang into the air and caught it. He tumbled to the ground, picked up two other stones and immediately began juggling them all, lifting them higher and higher in the air. Leopard and Bear, outraged at this interruption, both leapt up to snatch their boulder back, but once they were in the air, the Juggler began to juggle *them*, along with the stones. Stunned into stillness, Leopard and Bear were juggled higher and higher, until they were soaring in great arcs over the Sky Cricket pitch, over the world's last trees and caves.

Akshay's father huffed and strained every muscle to send them higher and higher still until, past the waves of wind washing past the highest leaves, Leopard got caught in a sticky patch of cloud, and she did not fall back to earth.

And with one last push, Akshay's father sent Bear in the grandest arc yet, out beyond the world, until he got caught by the crescent moon, and he did not fall back to earth.

The boulders were the only things to fall. The clouds, no longer disturbed by flying boulders and bone bats, skipped across the waves of wind washing past the highest leaves, on the edge of the world. No ice or bone fell on the village, and the villagers looked up in wonder and relief. The Juggler collapsed in exhaustion.

Clouded Leopard and Moon Bear were not to be stopped, however. They continued to play Sky Cricket, now firmly planted in the heavens, but Moon Bear exchanged his tree trunk bat for lunar lumber, while Clouded Leopard replaced her elephant bone for a bat of solid thunder. No longer earthbound, they used the closest stars as balls, and the boundary was the farthest stardust ring of the galaxy.

After that night, whenever there was an August crescent moon, Akshay was proud to lead his family and the villagers of Chail up the stairs, stone by stone, that wound up and around the hill, until they could hear the waves of wind washing past the highest leaves, out beyond the world, to the cricket pitch in the sky. They bore picnic baskets, blankets, and pillows, and resting on the pitch, turned their eyes to the night sky. Most of the game was played too high in the heavens for them to see, but they kept score by counting the shooting stars. Their houses and shops no longer threatened, the villagers rested easy—or at least most of them. Only the Astronomer remained restless, pacing by his telescope night after night, wondering what he would do now that he knew that the stars were just playthings.

VOYAGE STORY

Augusto Luiz Facchini

And as in the way of dreams, the boy did not remember how he came to be there or why he was there to begin with, but he was there, among the clouds, and he could feel the wind, viscerally, fluttering the scarf of his navy blue boy scouts' uniform, wooshing past his gangly arms and legs, cool and full of trepidation. There was the moon, this he will remember, pallid white and ghostly, bathing the endless cloudscape in ethereal light, so that everything was aglow like a specter, and he, alone, stood underneath the endless vast of darkness and stars lost in uncertainty, a witness to nothing. Yet he knew he was in the Dream. But soon, there was a sound, like a beating drum, thundering through the expanse, and as is in the way of dreams, the clouds reshaped themselves, their vaporous forms yielding to the appearance of a magnificent steed, pearly white with a mane and tail of air and light, with eyes that shone blacker than the blackest açaí berry, and legs that were as long as the sadness of life. And the wind was in its mane and the horse glided to him like cold water, and pressed his snout against the boy's cheek tenderly, and the boy knew the horse and loved it all at once, deeply.

"Dream," said the boy, for he knew that to be the horse's name, for it resonated inside of him like an old song he'd heard so often before that it sang itself to him without provocation or cause. "I came here to look for something, but I forgot what it was."

"You will remember it in time, Dearest Dreamer. Do you remember your name?" The boy thought and thought but this he couldn't remember either. He became frustrated and kicked at the ephemeral mist at his feet, only to see it wisp away in the shape of countless dandelion puffs, hovering away in the wind and into the endless night. The horse named Dream touched his forehead to the boy's, tenderly, and the boy embraced the Dream, and began to cry.

"Do not be sad, Dearest Dreamer," spoke the Dream, "your name is your own, to shape yourself. As is the water and the winds, and the clouds and the night sky, and the yellow of the mangoes on the tree, and the loneliness that we all carry in our hearts. For I am your Dream." So the boy made up his own name on the spot.

"Voyage," he said. "My name is Voyage."

They galloped through the land. On the back of his horse made of clouds, Voyage clung to the Dream, and they charged through rolling hills of green, whispering rivers, flowery vales, through mountain and forest, across desert and sea, over the day and through the night, and on and on they went until they came to a snowy-white expanse where the motes of soft fallen snow hung frozen in the air like ornaments and a singular barren tree, black as the Dream's dark eyes, reached its branches towards the ashen sky, standing silent and sentinel and utterly alone, stark against the infinite pale.

"Dream," said Voyage, "Why have you brought me here? Is this what I am looking for?" The boy dismounted and brushed away the wisps of snow that hung in the air before him, watched as they turned into butterflies and flitted away. The tree loomed, so big and monumental before him, like an obelisk or a disapproving parent, and yet was impossibly far.

"Only you can decide that, Dearest. I can only take you where you will to go."

"I feel like something bad has happened here."

"Perhaps something has."

"It's cold here, Dream. I'm scared. I don't want to stay. Take me away from this place."

"As you wish, my Dearest."

The boy rode his horse made of clouds through the world again. He wanted to ride and ride forever, and for the ride never to end. He embraced the horse named Dream around its neck, buried his face in its mane and whispered, "I love you," but whether the Dream heard him or not over the sound of its own thundering hooves, Voyage could not be sure, for he heard no reply. The sound of beating hoofbeats echoing in the dark became grinding steel, footsteps and hurried voices calling, the roar of engines, the vibrations of rumbling industry: they had come at last to a train station, where people in vests and long coats carried umbrellas and briefcases, all standing on the platform waiting for a train that churned far down the tracks that wound infinitely into the night.

"My mother is here," said Voyage, and she was, sitting on a bench with her stitching needle in hand and his torn stuffed monkey on her lap, and though he couldn't see her face, he remembered when the monkey, who he'd named Seu Macaco, ripped at the neck, bleeding white stuffing everywhere, and he had panicked for he thought his beloved friend was dead.

"She is indeed," said the Dream.

Voyage bounded across the platform to reach her, but with the hiss of steam and a sharp whistle, the train arrived on its tracks at the platform and the conductor yelled "All Aboard!" and the faceless multitudes of people and their briefcases and umbrellas became a torrent in front of him and no matter which way he turned and went there was no passing them, always one or another got in the way, jostling him about and he lost sight of his mother on the bench, and when he could see it again, she was gone.

"Dream!" he called, for he could not see the horse made of clouds, "Dream, help me!"

"I am here, Dearest." The voice came from behind him. The boy flung his arms around the Dream and wept.

"Dream, I lost her!" cried the boy. "She was just here, and I lost her."

"Take heart, Dearest Dreamer," said the Dream, "it is only a dream, after all."

"I want to wake up again," said the boy. The horse was silent, and dropped his head. Then the conductor called out to the empty station, "Last call! All Aboard!"

The boy rushed over to the conductor, who was stepping into the carriage, his hand on the rail, the black of his black shoe on the step that divides the known and the unknown, and as he looked at the boy, his face was familiar, a face he'd seen and known before, but he could not place it, as it was in the way of dreams.

"Mister," said Voyage, "Where does this train go?"

"It goes beyond," said the man and he tipped his hat with a smile and stepped into the car. The engine gave a hooting cry and billowed smoke from its chimney, and the wheels began to screech against the tracks.

"Beyond what?" cried the boy as he ran after the train.

"Beyond here," said the man, "and everywhere and nowhere."

"Is my mom in there?" called the boy. Already the train was beyond reach. He stopped running as he reached the end of the platform. The tracks extended past the station into a murky black void where the earth crumbled away to bits of chocolate chip cookie, floating in a vacuum, and the train chugged forward into the abyssal dark.

"She's waiting for you there," called the man. Voyage could just see him waving his cap goodbye. "They all are."

He stood and watched the train disappear. He wiped his wet face with the back of his arm. Behind him, he could hear the soft hoofsteps of the Dream approaching.

"Dream," said Voyage, "I want to wake up now."

"Indeed you must," said the horse, "though I will miss you terribly."

The boy closed his eyes tightly. Then he flung them open again. He was still there. "Can you help me?"

"No," said the Dream, "I wish I could, my Dearest."

The boy closed his eyes tightly once again. He inhaled deeply and tried to remember being awake. He tried opening his eyes again, but nothing happened. He heard a rhythmic chime sound around him, like the call of a night bird. He heard susurrant voices, though he could not make out their words, only whispers in the wind.

"Why can't I wake up?"

"This you must remember."

"I don't."

"Dearest, you must try."

"I feel as though something bad has happened."

"Perhaps it has."

"Just tell me."

"Dearest, I wish I could. But you are the dreamer, and I am only your Dream."

"I was looking for something. I forgot what it was. Dream, take me away from here. I don't like this place. There's something scary about it."

They rode and rode and rode. They rode through the parking lot sequestered behind the convenience store and the derelict building that used to be a flower shop, where, when had been a teenager, he had kissed another boy for the first time. They rode past the cemetery where he had stood awkwardly, unsure what to do with his hands, at his grandfather's funeral, as he watched the pallbearers lower the casket into the ground. They rode past the crowded city streets and the tall buildings made of shining glass and the indifferent cars crawling along under neon signs, and there was the dirty alleyway, littered with broken glass and plastic bags filled with trash that sang their song in the buzzing of flies, the alley where he had, a stupid twenty-something in a band t-shirt and torn up jeans, tried something that someone claimed was LSD and ended up puking in a dumpster while his friends laughed at him. Finally they came to a house, stately and impossibly tall and, as is in the way of dreams, sitting on top of a lily pad, floating in a pond among giant koi fish that lazily circled beneath the surface of the clear water. Ladybugs as big as oxen stood at the edge of the lily pad and their eyes flashed in colors, red and blue—blue and red—red and blue. "This is where it happened," said Voyage.

"This is where it happened," said Dream.

Already Voyage could feel light and weightless, and could see the colors of the dream melting like watercolor washed away from canvas. Voyage looked around for something familiar to anchor himself to. He could hear a chiming sound. Parakeets fluttering in the air beeped at him accusingly, then burst into iridescent bubbles. There was also a murmur of voices—the fish were in solemn consultation, but he could not decipher their underwater garbling.

He dismounted and walked along the lily pad, feeling it sink slightly underneath his steps, though his feet did not get wet as they sank into water. The koi fish with their rosy patterns, eyed him suspiciously and prattled on. His hair began to levitate, and soon his shoe laces too, and the scarf of his navy blue boy scouts' uniform fluttered away from him and though he tried to snatch it, he could not grasp it and it flew away into the wind.

He peered into the window of the strange house. He was there, a man, an adult man, in his too-small work T-shirt from a catering job over a decade ago and his pinstriped boxer shorts, with no shoes, lying on the kitchen floor, the orange juice he had been pouring spilled all over the granite counter and on the Mexican tile, the little white pills still floating upon it like tiny little boats, and there were people around him, they were saying something, the air was electric, urgent, and he tried to make out their words, but the window was melting away and his feet were beginning to hover into the air from the lily pad, an unseen force pulling him up as though he were a balloon accidentally released at an amusement park.

He tried to grab something to hang on and pull himself down, but as he grasped the window sill, it turned to paint in his hands and the droplets, like murky colored dew, hovered away.

"Dream!" the boy called, desperately flailing for anything to hold. "Dream, help me!" The horse galloped fiercely. The boy could see him charging towards him, but he was not fast enough. He was floating, careening into the sky. He could see the Dream racing towards him, but fading away. Everything was getting smaller and darkness encroached around him. He was spinning. He couldn't catch his breath. His arms and legs thrashed into the emptiness, finding nothing to cling to. "Dream!" his voice echoed into the vacuous nothing, and he watched the horse made of clouds blink out of sight, the last pinpoint of light that he could see before he was subsumed into the dark.

And so he was alone. Spinning in an endless void and utterly alone. He closed his eyes and wished he could wake up once more and then all at once he understood. The blackest black around him. The cold and empty solitude. All the sickness and sadness of all his years weighing upon him. He was no longer a little boy in his navy blue boy scouts' uniform, but a man, out of time and space, at the edge of the beyond.

Rumbling thunder. No, he realized. Hoofbeats. There—in the depth of his own darkness, Dream was coming for him. The horse made of clouds shone pearly white, all air and light, and charged for him heedlessly. It had never abandoned him, it had never given up.

He found himself once again in snow, at the roots of the solitary black tree. Dream lay on the ground, heaving, his mane and tail evaporating into white smoke into the air. Voyage knelt beside him. The boy cradled the horse's weary head in his lap, stroked its mane, and let his tears fall and turn into snowflakes, and snowflakes to butterflies.

"Dream, please don't go."

"I'm so sorry, Voyage."

"I'm still so lost."

"You will find your way. Do you remember your name?"

"I do. But it doesn't matter anymore. Voyage is my name now."

"It's a nice name."

"I'll miss you."

"I'll miss you too, Dearest."

"I'm not a little boy."

"No, you're not."

"I tried to— I mean I wanted to—"

"Yes, you did."

"Why did I do it? That was so stupid. Why, why did I do it?"

"You were very sick and very sad. You didn't want to hurt anymore. I only wish I had been there to comfort you, Dearest."

Voyage lowered his head and wept. He clutched Dream to him as closely as he could. He could see the pearly white light fading gray. The black eyes that were once blacker than the blackest açaí berry turning ashen pale.

"Dearest," said the Dream, "You have to wake up now."

"I can't," said Voyage. "I don't know how."

"You do. You must."

"I don't want to leave you."

"Dearest, I wish we could forever ride over the vales and clouds and sea. I would carry you to the stars and to the moon if that is what you wished. But dreams must end, Dearest Dreamer. Do not be sad. It is you who must carry me now as you drift through the world and gather the little joys you find along the long sadness of life. When you think of me, I'll be there, Dearest. I'll be there always."

He could hear it now. The doctors talking in their recondite language. The rhythmic beeping of machines pulsating. The electric hum of overhead fluorescent lights. Voyage took a last, longing look at the black tree. Towering and isolated, it stood timeless in the empty cold, witness to nothing and everything all at once. This was, after all, what he had been looking for all along.

"Goodbye," he said and closed his eyes. He felt the Dream melt away from him in his hands, evaporating into the shadow of a whisper. He felt the light surge over him like a waterfall, felt himself surrender to it. Warmth, radiance. Tears streaked down his face and he could feel their caress on his skin.

And as the milky twilight of consciousness washed over him, this Dream swirled into an eddy at the secret shores of memory, to be a whispered echo at the edge of sleep, a relic of a forgotten story, ephemeral as breath turning into vapor in the wintertime air. As is in the way of dreams.

MEL'S ROCK PILE

J.J. Stewart

In the loneliest corridor of the Eye of Jupiter space port, surrounded by faulty neon and un-recycled bio-cylinders, hidden from the trendier and more useful shops, rests Mel's Rock Pile: Antiques and DNA Sequencing.

It was the type of dim, useless shop that no one ever saw appear and no one ever knew how it stayed in business.

It was a scam.

It was antiquated and old.

It couldn't possibly exist.

It absolutely existed.

It was an urban legend.

Uppers—who occasionally saw sunlight and hydroponic fruit—believed Mel's was a myth. A VR fantasy created by people too bored to live in the real world. It was a lie meant to cut holes in Uppers' pockets and filter stolen credits down to the greedy fingers of the Lowers.

To the Lowers, Mel's was the final lottery for the station's desperate population. It was said that, if you were willing to pay, you could hold the chance to change the very fabric of your existence. It was magic, if such a thing could exist in Jupiter's orbit. Everyone knew someone who had a cousin who had dated someone who had dared the shop. Everyone knew that to enter Mel's meant coming out *changed*. Sometimes those people died. The Lowers' bedtime stories were full of horrific and splashy deaths laid at Mel's door. Tales of sliced oxygen hoses, failed magno-boots that cast their owners into the black void, tumbling endlessly for all time, or worse. Except one or two tales, which told of unfathomable riches; instant elevation to the highest of Upper echelons. But those stories were very few and very far between.

Mel herself, it was said, was a keen woman. Thin and sarcastic and wrapped warmly in layers of fall-colored homespun. She, like the diesel-scented corridors and alleys, was a fixture of the Lowers. The Eye of Jupiter would cease its storms before Mel left her Rock Pile. Mostly, what she did was wait. She was good at waiting.

Kyrzak, with his flashing eyes and messy hair, was very impatient. He slipped in and out of the Lowers' gangs, gossiping Aunties, and family units like a fish through water. He'd seen a fish, once, in a decrepit VR Suite that had been stuck replaying an Ancient Earth nature vid.

He'd found himself identifying with the recorded fish, flitting and shimmering through its endless stream. Looping over and over through still and placid waters. He'd gone back, week after week, mesmerized, until the Tres Terra gang discovered the broken Suite and co-opted it as an outdoor experience for their Haze addicts. That had been a month ago, and Kyrzak could still see the bright silver scales of the animal whenever he closed his eyes. He sighed and twitched his cap more firmly over his ears. It was cold. The pre-dawn cleaning steamers before the Kilowatt Festival always left the Lowers a bit chillier than the 24-hour 76 degrees that the Station promised prospective immigrants.

"Yo, Kyr!" A boy slid along the wall and slouched next to him. His clothes were similar to Kyrzak's. The boy gnawed at a ragged cuticle and then wiped the wet digit on his sleeve, leaving a faint smudge on already gray cloth.

"Sammi," Kyrzak nodded.

They shoved their shoulders together and then settled into a comfortable slouch. The two stared over the guardrail down to the tier below. Morning baking smells drifted up to the two friends. Sammi kicked his heel against the smooth wall. Kyrzak breathed and watched the memory of his fish glint behind his eyes.

"Kilowatt Festival tonight," Sammi said. He glanced at his friend and twisted a button in his fingers.

"Yup."

"You going?"

"Dunno. Maybe."

Sammi shoved his hands deep into his pockets. He gripped the lining, making his fists bulge strangely on his thighs.

"So . . ." he began.

Something was happening for Sammi, Kyr thought. *Something that might, possibly, not be utterly boring.*

"It's just . . ." Sammi began, as usual, in the middle of his sentence. Like the thought happened in his head and only occasionally lept out of his mouth. "Cinco Terra offered to let me join. And . . . Well, if I join, I won't be back on this level. You know Cinco, they never come above 1k."

Kyrzak raised an eyebrow. "You gonna join?"

Sammi shrugged. "What else am I gonna do? Mamman said there's no more room in the unit now that I'm out of school and Cytia's kids are out of nursery."

Kyrzak shrugged.

"You want to join up with me?" Sammi drummed his fingers unrhythmically on the handrail. "It could be k-rads, you know? Two of us? Joining Cinco and exploring the Deeps? Maybe we'd find one of the Original's units! Or discover a pure CadNi p-cell! We'd be Uppers if we found that! Absolutely rolling in it! You wanna come? The two of us champions ruling the deeps?"

"A pure CadNi? More like find a trapdoor to the waste tunnels, you mean," Kyr scoffed. He had been wrong. Sammi wasn't up to anything interesting at all. He sighed to himself. *Just more of the same old work 'til you die. Don't matter who for.* "The Deeps ain't nothing more than picked over bones, Sammi. Cinco is desperate for bodies 'cause they keep running out of workers to grease the machines. Not me, Watto, I'm not joining Cinco."

"Oh," Sammi's face fell. He kicked his toe out over the edge. "So what are you gonna do? Heating? Air? Garbage?"

"None of that," Kyrzak tugged at the hem of his dark jacket. "I ain't interested in dying before I get to live. All that work is instant death."

Sammi blew out a whistle. "You going for Catering? Uppers Service One?" He started laughing. "C'mon Kyr! You almost had me! You? In Service One? You don't have the talk! And I never seen you sit still for two minutes, much less all of those hours-long dinners the Uppers do. No, seriously, what you going to do? It's Kilowatt Festival. Gotta choose."

"Maybe I'll join the Spacers," Kyr grumbled.

"You full of jokes, man!" Sammi cracked a huge grin and slapped Kyr on the shoulder. "Hey, remember back in Form Five and they took us all to forty-third level to see the Eye and you up-chucked all over the window because you were so scared of the empty space?"

"Shut up, Sammi," Kyr said.

"You know where Spacer's work, right?"

"Shut up, Sammi."

"What's all that stuff that surrounds Spacer's? All day, every day? Only separated by a couple of layers of plasmo? What's it called? Oh, yeah, *Space!*"

"Shut *up*, Sammi!"

"Heh, Spacer's. You had me, Kyr. Seriously, what you gonna do if not one of the work crews? You know there ain't no room for us in the family units after the festival."

Kyr banged his head with the heel of his hand. He could feel something, throbbing behind his eyes. Some nameless feeling, building in the space of his chest behind his lungs. His hands curled into fists. He closed his eyes. He could see his glinting, silver fish, many centuries dead, flashing through cool water, endlessly circling, spending eternity going round and round until the crystals degraded enough to wipe their recording forever.

"I . . ."

"Yeah? What are you going to do?"

"I'm . . ." Kyrzak's brain fizzed. He could almost feel each dreary photon from the buzzing fluorescent lights above, landing painfully against his skin, setting his molecules on fire.

"I'm going to see Mel," he announced.

"Kyr don't joke, you can't!" Sammi straightened, alarmed. "She's a monster, Kyr! It's not like the stories. My Aunty Gythic's second husband had a nephew who went to see Mel and he told her that she . . ."

Kyrzak pushed off from the wall. "I'm going to Mel's," he interrupted. "She's just people, Sammi. She'll tell me . . ."

"She'll tell you what?" Sammi asked.

Kyr paused for a moment and then shook his head.

"She'll have something to say, and I'm going to listen," he announced. He shook himself and marched off, relieved, as ever, to be moving, to have something to *do*. He stopped at the doors to the lift and looked back at his childhood friend. "You wanna come?" he asked.

"I . . ." Sammi clutched at the collar of his coat, bought fairly new for his Kilowatt Festival choice. He pressed himself against the wall of the corridor that had been their entire lives.

The door to the lift squeaked open on old, rusty runners, and the weak orange light of the car spilled out onto the floor between them. Kyr took one last look at his friend and then stepped into the car. "Later. I guess," he said.

The door started to shake itself closed as Kyr punched in the number for the level where Mel's shop waited—1600—as far down as anyone could go without special breathing equipment. Sammi frantically pushed himself off the wall and ran towards the closing door. "Kyr, hold the door!" But he was too late, the door closed and he heard the hissing of the car as its magnets activated and took it away.

The lift dropped, twisting with the other lift tubes into an immense braid that stretched from one end of the station to the other. Kyr tapped his fingers on his thigh. Eventually, a soft chime sounded and the old door creaked open on a corridor very much like the one he had left. It had the same lighting, same stale air, same industrial carpeting. The only thing that differed was, where his home tier hummed with small shops and gossip, this one felt abandoned.

As he stepped out of the door, he hesitated. The station was cylindrical, so either way, he'd end up there eventually, but he'd hate to spend so much energy going right, if Mel's Rock Pile was actually ten meters to the left. He shrugged and headed left on the premise that it had always *seemed* shorter to go counterclockwise. He walked past old-fashioned home units and pawn shops and convenience stores that never bothered to try and hide the expiration dates on their protein packs. He passed a few people in the corridor, quiet and drab and eager to get from point A to point B with as little time as possible passed in between.

This had better not be boring, he thought to himself.

Usually, everything was boring. Every minute of every day was eternally boring. He could nearly feel the seconds scratch his face as they sped past. Still, he trudged onwards. He had definitely gone much, much further than ten meters and there was still no sign of Mel's Rock Pile. He grumbled to himself and plodded on, counting his steps to keep himself occupied. At 1,000 steps, he got too bored to keep counting. Some time after that, the corridor finally began showing some sort of life. The hole-in-the-wall shops began illuminating their signs. First with small, warm-wave strips, then with fancier spotlights or simul-torches, and then with ever-growing amounts of blinking neon colors. Kyr puzzled over the difference between the past curve of the corridor and this one. It was almost like all of the life of the entire level was concentrated in this small section and the rest of the corridor had been sucked dry to sustain it.

Finally, nearly 6,000 steps from where he'd exited the elevator, he saw a sign, illuminated in red neon, that read:

Mel's Rock Pile: Antiques and DNA Sequencing

A smaller sign:

Loans accepted, dreams made

Well, Kyr thought to himself, *I'm here.* He hesitated for a moment and then pushed the shop door open and slid inside.

The interior of the shop was full of heavy furniture and small lamps of warm, illegal, incandescent bulbs that cast exciting shadows across the floor. There were no overhead lights. The door swung closed and shut out the constant hum of the station and its multitude of levels. For the first time in his entire life, Kyr felt alone. It was utterly and completely silent. And it felt *exciting.* The hair on his arms prickled as he slowly gazed around and took in the contents of the shop. For, as advertised on the sign outside, Mel's Rock Pile was full of rocks.

Beneath every shaded lamp, spilling out of countless drawers, piled high on antique cake stands, and mounded waist-high upon the floor in sweeping piles, lay rocks. Big rocks, small rocks, polished rocks, unpolished stones, diamonds, rubies, tiger-eye, cerulean spheres, geodes, shale . . . A million rocks from a million worlds gleamed, sparkled, and shone from every corner of the shop. Here and there, pale fossils peaked from behind casks of turquoise and lapis lazuli. Fragments of petrified trees, carefully wired back together, claimed the far walls. Kyr took an involuntary step further into the shop and stumbled, his feet sinking, for the very first time in his life, into dry, powdery sand. It lay in a deep pit that shifted as he moved, submerging his feet further with every step. He shook his foot, trying unsuccessfully to dislodge the unexpected sand from in between his toes and back out the holes in his sock.

"Well. You're here." A voice, paper-dry, floated from the back counter and broke the silence. "And I suppose you're not going to pay for the sand you'll track away?"

A thin figure emerged from behind the huge counter and leaned her elbows on the glass surface. Kyr glanced away from his feet. *Brown*, he thought. Short brown hair, buzzed as close as his own. A chocolate-colored scarf over a long, orangy-brown, knee-length knitted sweater and cream-colored trousers. She was all the glorious tones of an Earth that he'd never seen. All except for her pale blue eyes, glinting from underneath her furrowed brow.

"Pay? For this?" Kyr asked. He gave up trying to keep from sinking into the deep sand and slogged awkwardly towards the woman behind the counter. "You mean this stuff is going to *stay* with me? I don't want this! It's uncomfortable!"

"It's sand. That's what it does. Unless you're making glass and then it does something else entirely."

"Uh, sure. Yeah," Kyr said. He made his way out of the sand and stood on threadbare carpeting in front of the counter. He shook his feet again, one after the other, trying to drain the clinging stuff from his flimsy station shoes. "How do I get rid of it?"

"*Tch,*" Mel clucked her tongue. "Shouldn't have walked through the sand pit if you didn't want sand. Hold still." She flicked a switch on the counter. A whirring sounded through the shop and the floor started to vibrate. Kyr yelped as all of the particulates in his shoes, socks, and clinging to his feet suddenly discorporated, jumped five inches backwards, rematerialized on the carpet, and then flowed like mercury back to the sand pit.

"What was that?!" he screeched.

"Magnets, a sedimentary sifter, and a lot of practice," Mel counted off the aspects on her fingers. "You're welcome, by the way." She sniffed, pointedly.

"Oh. Uh . . . Thanks," Kyr muttered.

"So, let's try again," Mel said. "Well. You're here."

"Yes, I am."

He looked around at the shop. From up front, he could see even more rocks and stones behind the counter piled into a huge mound. These were all lustrous, deep-gray, smoothly polished stones that glinted enticingly. The holographic fish flickered behind his eyes. Kyr would have been willing to bet his last credit that they would make the most satisfying *click-clack* sound if someone were to slide down the pile.

"Well, *you're* here, Kyr," Mel said for the third time.

"Yeah. I'm here," Kyr agreed. For all of the weirdness when he walked in, he might have just stayed in his home corridor if this is the type of talk that was going to happen.

"Aren't you going to ask how I know who you are?" Mel asked.

"Do you know who I am?"

"Yes."

"Well, I know who you are."

"Yes, but you're supposed to know who I am," Mel snapped. "There are two billion humans on this station and you're not even the littlest bit curious or surprised that I can, apparently, not only know all two billion of them by name, but can recognize them without ever having actually met them before?"

Kyr pondered that for a moment.

"I mean," he said. "If you had a bio-reader on the shop door, you'd never need to remember everyone. We're all tagged and scanned every day. So, you know, it's not that impressive."

"Yes, but that's not what I did," Mel protested.

"Yeah, but you could have done it that way. So, you know . . . Whatever," Kyr shrugged.

Mel rubbed her temples with her fingers. "What do you want, Kyr?" She looked like she'd opened a package of protein rations and had found a splitting headache instead of her evening meal. Most of Kyr's teachers, once they got over the excitement of his initial test scores, had worn the same look.

"Kilowatt Festival tonight," Kyr said. He rubbed his thumb along the tips of his fingers. His fingers felt hard, cold, and foreign.

"Yes," Mel answered. She took a sip from an ancient metal water bottle.

Kyr kicked at the carpet. It was so *boring* to have to explain it with words. It took so *long* to push the actual words from his actual brain and out his actual mouth. And then, it was even odds that anyone would actually listen to the words without taking a really long, boring, time about it. And then the time it took them to answer back . . . He shuddered and kicked the carpet again.

The silence lengthened in the muffled shop. Somewhere, away in the darkness, Kyr could hear a slow, methodical ticking. He'd never heard a mechanical clock before. It reminded him of the Core Readout that counted down every moment of every day that he could hear even in his most dreamless sleep.

"Kyr," Mel asked again, "why are you here?"

Kyr felt a hard, painful lump in his chest. The same thing he'd felt ever since seeing that stupid fish in that stupid broken VR Suite. He opened his mouth but couldn't force any air out of his chest. He fisted his hands in his pockets and screwed his eyes shut.

Mel waited. She was very good at it.

"What . . ." Kyr began and then shook his head. "How am I supposed to live with all of *this?*" He waved his arm wildly around his head. "What am I supposed to do with myself?"

Mel's lips lifted in a quick, tight smile. A question had been asked, which meant that an answer was inevitable. Without looking, she reached out a hand and picked up a piece of polished red jasper. She flicked it between her fingers, tumbling it over and over.

"What do you want to do?" she asked. She placed the jasper on the counter with a sharp click. Then, she pulled open a drawer in the counter and pulled out a small green pyramid of jade, a purple amethyst cylinder, and a small lump of pyrite. She set each one on the glass countertop and poked them into a rough circle.

"I don't know, that's why I'm here." Kyr bent down until his eyes were on the same level as the stones. His breath fogged the glass counter.

"Fair enough," Mel answered. She set down a smooth slice of obsidian in the middle of the circle. "But what do you want? Not what do you want to do, but what do you, Kyr, want?"

Kyr straightened and glared at Mel's merchandise. Slowly, he realized that every single stone, the ones glimmering under lamplight, the ones piles haphazardly in corners and into drawers, even the ones that had been wired or glued into fantastical shapes—each one was no larger than what could be comfortably fit into a hand or slipped into a pocket during a solitary ramble along a beach or mountain hike. Each one was slightly different, slightly unique. How long had it taken to collect all of these stones? The questions forced their way into his mind. What type of person would collect millions of small rocks, carry them to a distant space station, and then . . . open a shop? To sell these rocks to . . . whom? No one came here, at least not more than once.

"What do you want, Kyr?" Mel asked again. Her voice was gentle, but the command was not.

"I . . ." Kyr paused and then, in a rush, said, "I don't want it to be boring anymore! I can't stand it. The same conversations, the same rations, the same corridors, the same people, the same brains . . . Day after day, it's always the same! It's so *boring!*"

"Ah," Mel said. With one hand, she swept the rocks in front of her into a tight huddle. Then, with the other hand, she spread them out again. "I can help with that."

"All of these rocks," Kyr wondered as he stepped up to the counter and reached out a trembling finger to the obsidian piece, "are they . . ." He reached into the back of his mind for a word rarely used and never believed. "Are they . . . magic?"

"Wooo! What a question! You used the 'M' word! I didn't

think anyone on this station even knew that word existed anymore!" Mel crowed. "Yes, they are magic, incredibly old and powerful magic. And at the same time, no, don't be ridiculous, there's no such thing as magic."

"What type of answer is that?" Kyr demanded.

"It's a true answer, for one," countered Mel. "All rocks, at least, all of these rocks *are* magic," she continued. "But their magic is very specific."

"What do you mean?" Kyr asked. He poked again at the obsidian. It didn't feel any different than the corridor back home, smooth and cool. The only real difference seemed to be the color.

"That one, that you just touched, grants any wish, as long as the holder made that wish at 3:30 pm on any Tuesday in 1983."

"1983?" Kyr asked.

"The year 1983. That would have been about," Mel tipped her head back, counting. "300 years ago? Roughly. There have been at least five different calendar changes since then, so it's hard to tell."

"What about this one?" Kyr touched the red jasper.

"Oh, that's a very wicked stone," Mel grumped. "It would set any witch that touched it on fire."

"Witches?" Kyr said.

"An old religion. And also an old non-religion," Mel replied. "But it only works on dry land. When I found it on the last beach of Old Earth, it had been lost in the ocean for at least a thousand years. I stuffed it in a sealed jar of oil until we could move here, out in the depths of space." She plucked the red stone from Kyr's fingers. "Oh yes, we're old enemies, this stone and I." She dropped the stone into a drawer on her side of the counter and closed it with a snap. "Eventually, I'll need to shove it out of an airlock so that it can spin in space for a billion years, but I enjoy watching its frustration."

"All of these rocks are magic?" Kyr asked. He looked around again. The mounds of rocks that had, just moments ago, seemed so interesting and soothing, now seemed sinister and dangerous. He looked at the inviting pile of slick, dark gray silver behind Mel. He'd wanted to slide down it! For fun! What might have happened to him? "Are other things magic? Is everything magic under the right conditions?" He tugged at his collar. Were his clothes waiting for the specific moment to betray him?

"No, no, no," Mel tapped his knuckles. "Just stones. And just specific stones. I've found as many as I could and brought them here, where they can either be out of the way or put to use. Ah! Look at this fellow!" She held the amethyst cylinder to the light. Deep within its lavender heart, Kyr could almost believe he saw a white . . . something . . . glimmer.

"This beauty whispers sweet lullabies at midnight on the full moon of every month," she said. She kissed the stone and put it back on the counter.

"It doesn't murder anyone?" Kyr asked.

"Nope."

"That sounds . . . nice?" Kyr ventured.

"It's always nice when they aren't actively trying to murder anyone," Mel agreed.

"So, how does that help me?" Kyr asked. "It's the Kilowatt Festival. I'm supposed to choose my entire life tonight, and I don't see how some magical rocks will help with me destined to spend my whole entire life being completely and utterly bored!"

"Well," Mel began. "That's the whole point of the store. You get to choose a rock."

"You giving me some weird, oddly specific magic rock doesn't seem like much help!"

"What if a weird, oddly specific magic rock could stop you from ever experiencing boredom ever again?

Kyr paused. A throbbing, rushing sound thundered in his ears.

"What did you say?" He swallowed against his suddenly dry throat.

"How much are you willing to give up to never be bored again?"

"How much?" Kyr asked. His heart sank like a lift plummeting to the lowest livable levels. "Like, credits? I'm from the Lowers. You know how much I don't have."

"Did I ask for credits?" Mel asked.

"What else is there?"

"I want a year of your life."

"What?!" Kyr yelped. "No deal, Wheelo! Keep away from me!" He backed away from the counter.

"Relax, Kyr, I'm not going to hurt you," Mel plucked a small turquoise stone egg from a pocket and placed it on the counter. "I need one year of your life, but I'm perfectly happy to take it from the very end. You'll just die a year earlier than you would have, normally, if you had stayed in your corridor and never entered my shop.

Kyr stumbled backwards into the sand pit.

"Stay back! Don't you touch me!" He kicked out at her, sending a small cloud of sand scattering through the air between them.

"Think of it, would you really want that year?" Mel leaned

forward across the glass. "Lost in the Deeps with the Cinco? Or serving in one of the Uppers endless cocktail parties? Two hundred years serving on this station with no hope for anything different from day to day? Don't you think a single year from the very tail end of that life is worth never having to live that life at all?"

"Two hundred years?" Kyr asked. A tsunami of boring, beige days rose before him. He shuddered. "That's how long I've got?"

"Well, if you make this deal, one hundred and ninety-nine," Mel smiled at him.

He shuffled back onto solid ground, not feeling the grit inside his shoes.

"And which stone do I get?" Kyr asked.

"Nope, payment first," Mel said. She pushed back from the counter and crossed her arms. The small turquoise egg gleamed in the lamplight. Its sky-blue color seemed to swirl as Kyr watched.

"That's not fair!"

"It's my shop," she pointed out.

"Nuh-uh, not going to happen," Kyr crossed his arms and scowled at her.

"Alright," she said, "door's that way." She pointed behind him. "Have a good Kilowatt Festival, enjoy all the years ahead of you."

Kyr stood glowering at her. The silence stretched, broken only by the faint ticking Kyr couldn't place.

Mel raised her eyebrows at him. "Are you planning on just glaring at me or are you going to make a purchase? I've got other customers, you know."

"Who else is here?" Kyr demanded.

"*Tch,* I'm a busy woman," Mel replied. "There are two billion people on this station. I could have another customer at any moment." She sniffed. "Don't you have a Kilowatt Festival to get to? Big decisions ahead of you, after all." She licked her finger and rubbed a smudge off of the turquoise egg.

Kyr glanced back at the door and the rest of his life that waited on the other side.

"Fine, you can have a year of my life," he conceded. "But the very last year, nothing else!" He shook a finger at her.

"I wouldn't have it any other way," Mel said. She smiled, reached out, and tapped the stone egg against the counter. Kyr was incredibly surprised when it cracked open and, inside, there sat a tiny turquoise house that stood on chicken legs. The miniature house shook its legs and stretched up until it rubbed its chimney against Mel's palm.

"Good House," she murmured and dropped a kiss on its tiny roof. "Get to work, House," she said. The small house turned so that its front door faced Kyr. Tiny puffs of smoke appeared from its chimney as it appeared to contemplate him.

Kyr bent down so that his face was even with the house.

"What in the Deeps is this thing?" He asked.

"This is House," Mel said. "House, meet Kyr."

The House scratched at the counter top and cocked a window at Kyr. Then, without warning, the small front door burst inwards and a strong wind clutched at Kyr. It was like when he'd leapt from the stratosphere jumps when he was a kid. Except, instead of the wind pushing him away, the House's wind was pulling him towards the door. And it was getting stronger. He pushed against the counter to keep himself upright, but the wind clawed at him, grasping at his jacket, his hair, anything of him that it could possibly reach. He pushed against the sucking wind with all of his might, but felt himself bending, pulled into the door in the tiny house that he couldn't possibly fit through.

"Help me!" he screamed.

"This is the payment," Mel replied. She backed away from the counter, well away from the pulling wind. "It'll probably be over soon."

And then it was. The wind dropped abruptly and Kyr shoved himself from the counter. His feet skidded out from under him as he windmilled backward. He banged up against the petrified forest, smacking his elbow and the back of his head against the stone trees. Groaning, he stood up and rubbed his scraped hands.

"What the Eye was that?!" he demanded.

"Payment," Mel repeated.

The turquoise chicken house crouched beneath Mel's chin. It preened itself and smoke puffed steadily from its chimney. Kyr cautiously approached the counter.

"So now what?" he asked.

A spark gleamed in Mel's light blue eyes and she waved her hand grandly towards the rest of the store. "Now you get to choose! Select any stone you want. You can take any one of them that you want. It's yours."

"Any of them?" Kyr couldn't believe his ears. Any magic stone that he wanted and all he had to do was take it? That, certainly, wasn't boring.

"Any of them," Mel assured him. "Except for my little house, of course." House chirped sleepily and nestled further against Mel's chest.

"But how will I know which one to choose?"

"You'll know."

Kyr stumbled into the main area of the store. He gathered a handful of emeralds, examining each one carefully before letting them all slip through his fingers to drop back into their original pile. He polished a large piece of jasper, not the witch burning one, on his sleeve and rejected it. He touched diamonds and garnets before finding them too cold and unfriendly to keep. Daringly, he stepped behind the counter and threw himself on top of the pile of slick stones he'd noticed. They did, indeed, make an incredibly satisfying noise as he slid down them.

He tried to hide his giggle.

"Everyone slides down the hematite pile. I do it myself from time to time." Mel cocked her hip and leaned against the counter, watching him.

His eyes gleamed and he threw himself down the pile again.

Finally, a large globe of tiger-eye caught his eye. It was resting, by itself, in the basin of an old-fashioned banker's lamp, its gold and amber streaks shone like his own, personal, miniature Jupiter. He picked it up and it felt . . . good . . . in the cup of his palm.

"This one," he said. He brought it back for Mel's inspection.

"That one? Are you sure?" Mel asked.

"Absolutely. This is it," Kyr stated. He rubbed his thumb over the sphere and discovered a slight depression on one side that was exactly the right spot for his first knuckle to rest. "It's perfect," he breathed.

"Then that's the one for you," Mel agreed. She nodded to herself. "Alright, Kyr, that's a deal. We're done now."

"What magic does it do?" Kyr asked.

"Ah," Mel shrugged. She thumbed a smudge off of the glass counter in front of her. "Well, that's the thing, actually . . ."

"It's magic, isn't it?" Kyr demanded.

"Of course it's magic!" Mel said. "It's just . . ."

"What? Is it evil? Does it kill people?" Kyr clutched the tiger eye to his chest. It felt so good in his hands. He screwed his eyes shut, bracing himself.

"I'm not allowed to tell you what magic it has," Mel said.

"*What?*"

"I'm not allowed to . . ." Mel began.

"I heard you," Kyr interrupted. "But I don't understand. Don't you know?"

"Oh yes, I know," Mel said. "I know every single stone in here. But I'm not allowed to tell you. You have to find out on your own."

"But it could be anything!" Kyr protested. "It could even be something that might never happen again or something that could only happen a thousand years from now!"

"Yes, that's true," Mel agreed. "But I'm still not allowed to tell you."

"But that's not fair!" Kyr's breath came in ragged drags. His blood pounded in his ears.

"That's part of the magic, Kyr," Mel said gently. "All I can really tell you is three things: One, its magic hasn't happened yet. Two, its magic can affect you, personally, if you figure it out. And, finally, the stone's magic will never be discovered by doing anything, and I do mean anything, from your old life."

"What does that mean?" Kyr asked. "I can't wear these clothes again? I can't tie my shoelaces the same anymore?"

Mel looked at him with kindness in her eyes. "Not quite that drastic, but . . . Come on, Kyr. You're a very intelligent boy. You know where this is heading."

"I have to leave the station?" he asked.

"Only if you want to discover the magic of the tiger eye," she reassured him. "It's your choice. You can stay here and the rock will only ever be a rock, and you can go to the Kilowatt Festival and live your life. And, Kyr," she stressed. "I want you to know: that life?—a life on the station with your friends and family—is a perfectly nice and fine life. You don't *have* to go chasing the magic.

"But, if you want to discover any magic in your fine piece of tiger eye, you'll need to go out, away as far as you can, and never do anything the same way that you've been doing before this moment. Because the magic could be anything. It could happen at any time. It could be a wish or a word or a third cup of tea that you have on Old Earth on Sunday mornings."

"What's tea?" Kyr asked.

"You'll have to find out," Mel smiled at him. "Or not. It's up to you to figure out what your rock does. I'm just the shop person."

"What if I never figure it out?" Kyr asked. He held the tiger eye up to his face and looked deeply into its heart. "What if I miss my chance by five minutes or five steps?"

"Do you really think that's possible? You? The indefatigable Kyr?" Mel scoffed.

Kyr straightened away from the counter. He slipped the tiger eye into his coat pocket and tugged at his sleeves.

"No, that's never going to happen," he said confidently. "Never in a million, million years am I not going to figure this out."

He turned and marched towards the door of the shop. There was a shuttle leaving the station soon, there was *always* a shuttle leaving the station. He would be on it, no matter what. He pushed his way through the dirty shop door, turned right, and departed the corridor as quickly as his feet would carry him. His magic would wait for no one and he'd let no one, no one at all, stop him from finding something amazing. He had a rock, after all.

"Goodbye, Kyr." Mel stretched and sighed and tickled the tiny turquoise house until it shivered a leg and wriggled and purred at her. The silence of the shop descended again, broken only by the endless ticking of the clock hidden deeply in the shadows and the tiny scratching of a small stone house with chicken legs playing on a worn glass counter.

Mel tucked the house safely back inside his egg. She then pulled out a large, leather receipt book and scanned through the pages. She found the entry she wanted and drew a thin, black line through the words *Tiger Eye sphere, magical properties: none.*

Acknowledgments

Thank you to *Tanya Nicolaeva* for the original oil painting cover art. To *David Kirk* for generously offering his superb illustration skills. To all our advanced readers, especially and specifically *Patricia McMahon* and *Kalie Parker,* for their kind reviews. And to the numerous writers who submitted stories to this anthology, thank you for putting a little more whimsy out into the world! It takes a school of fish to confuse a shark.

9 798990 679832